COWBOY PERIL

Cowboy Peril

Cynthia Hickey

The Cowboys of Misty Hollow, Book 2

Cowboy and horses, what's not to love?

Chapter One

It had been a really bad year.

Parker Wells smoothed the sleek black pants over her hips and put on some rosy-colored lipstick. Stepping back, she smiled. It had been a while since she'd gone out with friends for some fun.

Her smile faded. Six months in fact. Fun hadn't seemed possible after the suspicious death of her parents. Before that, at their insistence, she'd complied with their wishes and told the man she couldn't marry him, breaking her heart into pieces. That was the last time she'd seen or heard from Colt, although rumor had it he was working on a horse ranch in the northern part of the state.

A horn honked outside, spurring her to move faster. She grabbed her purse, locked the apartment, and dashed down the stairs and out the door. A man on the porch jumped out of her way, muttering something under his breath. "Sorry." She kept moving, then slid into the front seat of Tanya's car. Through the front windshield, she gave the man a pert smile and a wave.

Take that, whoever you are.

"Ready to have some fun?" Tanya backed from the building.

"I'll try. I'm not really into the whole nightclub, bar scene."

"So, don't drink. Order some sparkling water. Dance a little. You've done nothing but work and stay to yourself since your parents died."

"They were killed."

Tanya sighed. "The police found no evidence of that, Parker."

"There is no way my father would've lost control on a road he's driven a million times." She refused to believe it. "He'd been very worried about something or someone. I heard him talking to my mother about…something. Although I couldn't hear their words, I could tell from his tone."

"Okay. Whatever you say."

At the club, they flashed their IDs at the doorman. "He with you?" The doorman jerked his chin past them.

Parker glanced back, noticing the man she'd almost barreled into her on the porch. "No." She gripped her friend's arm and pulled her into the club that was already pulsating with music. "Let's find a table."

"No, let's head to the bar. I want to be seen. I want to dance." Tanya pulled free and scurried toward two empty bar stools. "You'd better dance, too. After all, you broke up with Colt months ago. It's time to find someone new. With that inky hair and blue eyes, you're hard to miss."

What if she didn't want anyone else? She perched on the stool and ordered sparkling water. Her parents hadn't wanted her to marry a practically penniless cowboy, and she'd caved under the pressure. Now, they were dead, and Parker had no one.

"That man keeps staring at you." Tanya elbowed her.

Parker cut a sideways glimpse at a table in a dark corner. "I saw that man outside my apartment. He was wearing a hat that covered his eyes and had his head turned, but that's him."

"So?" Her friend shrugged. "Maybe he lives there, or maybe you just think it's the same guy."

"I've never seen him before. Something about him gives me the creeps."

"Go talk to him."

"No." She pulled her gaze away. A few minutes later, another side-eyed peek showed he still was staring in her direction. Why? There were plenty of other women in the club. Why keep his attention on someone who clearly wasn't interested? She should've stayed home and watched TV or read a book. "Excuse me."

Tanya nodded, then slid off her stool and asked a man to dance.

Parker pushed open the door to the women's restroom, taking refuge in the semi-quiet. The noise of the music had diminished. Only one other woman occupied a stall, and she left before Parker entered the adjacent one.

Heavy footsteps sounded, then paused outside her stall. Dirty work boots, the kind with steel toes.

"This is the women's restroom, sir." Her heartbeat quickened.

For several long, tense seconds, the man stood

there, before turning and leaving.

Parker's breath escaped in a rush. Her hands shook. If he'd mistakenly entered the wrong room, he'd have apologized. The man hadn't said anything—except for the sound of heavy breathing.

She inched open the stall door and peered out. Empty. She quickly washed her hands, then peeked through the door leading back to the club before opening it. No sight of the man with dirty boots. She hunted Tanya down on the dance floor. "I'm going to call for a ride."

"What? Why?" Her friend sent her dance partner an apologetic smile.

"A man came into the women's bathroom and stood outside the stall I was using. It freaked me out. I don't want to stay here."

Tanya studied her face for a minute, then nodded. "I'll take you home."

"No, you stay. Have fun. I'll have the doorman call me a cab." She gave her friend a quick hug. "I'm sorry. It's just I'm not ready yet."

"I understand, but are you sure?"

"Yes." Parker flashed a grin, then rushed for the entrance.

Less than fifteen minutes later, she sat in the back of a sedan heading to her apartment. When they arrived, she quickly paid the driver, darted inside the apartment building and up the stairs, then slammed her door and leaned against it. Maybe she was being a party-pooping ninny, but the whole evening had left her nerves on edge.

She washed off her makeup, donned some baggy shorts and an oversized tee-shirt, then sat on the sofa and turned on the television. Nothing could hold her attention for long. Wow, the guy had spooked her.

Sighing, she stood and padded to the front window overlooking the parking lot. A man stood under a streetlight; his features shadowed. An eerily familiar man. The guy from the porch, who'd watched her at the club. She was sure of it.

Giving a salute in her direction, he strolled down the sidewalk and out of sight. Parker's heartbeat sped up double time. As she stepped back from the window, she noticed Tanya's car parked out front. What? Her breath came in gasps, and she wiped moist palms on her shorts. Why would her friend be sitting in her car outside her apartment?

Plucking her keys from the table near the front door, Parker put them between her fingers as a makeshift weapon and crept down the stairs a lot slower than she had before. She glanced out the door, making sure no one was around before opening it, then ran to the car.

"Tanya?" She knocked on the window. Her friend sat slumped over the steering wheel. Had she had too much to drink and come to Parker's with the intention of staying the night? Parker did live closer to the club.

When her friend didn't respond, she opened the driver side door and gave her a shake. Tanya's head lolled back revealing a slit across her throat. Pinned to her blouse was a bloodstained sheet of paper. Through the blood, Parker read, "Your parents ruined me. They've paid for their sin. Now, it's your turn."

Parker stumbled backward, clapping a hand over her mouth. Her best friend was dead, and it was somehow her fault. Tanya was murdered. How could this happen? The note said he was coming after her. She couldn't stay. But where could she go? She whipped around and clamored back upstairs to her apartment. She had to call the police, pack, get her hands on some money. Parker needed a plan. The note. She needed the note. It was the proof that her parents hadn't just died in an accident.

Oh, Tanya. She sat on the bed and covered her face with her hands. Why her? She couldn't have anything to do with whatever this man thought Parker's parents had done. Was she simply a message?

With shaking hands, Parker picked up her cell phone and dialed 911. The operator told her to stay in her apartment and lock her door, not opening it for anyone but the police. Staying on the phone, she moved back to the front window to wait for their arrival.

Rain fell from the sky. Flashing blue and red lights broke through the rain as two squad cars pulled into the parking lot. Four officers, guns drawn, approached Tanya's car. Since Parker had fled and left the driver's door open, it didn't take them long to assess the situation. In unison, all four officers turned and stared up at her apartment window. One peeled away and entered the building.

Parker hung up the phone and waited for his knock.

Chapter Two

Parker stepped back and let the officer in. Her legs shook hard enough to make her wobble.

"Have a seat, Miss." The officer took her by the arm and helped her to the sofa. "Take a deep breath, then tell me what happened."

She started with the bar and the man coming into the bathroom, then seeing the man standing on the curb, and ended with finding Tanya's body. "Why would someone angry with me kill my friend?"

He frowned and tilted his head. "Why would someone be angry with you?"

She told him of her suspicions regarding her parents' death. "Now, he's after me. You read the note, right?"

"Note?" He frowned.

"The one pinned to Tanya's blouse."

"We saw no note, ma'am."

"But..." It had been there. She'd seen it with her own eyes. "The killer came back and got it. That must be what happened." Her mouth dried. "The note said, 'Your parents ruined me. They've paid for their sin.

7

Now, it's your turn.'"

"What does that mean?"

"I don't know, but it confirms that my parents were killed. The precinct should have the file on their accident."

"I recognize the name. No foul play was detected in their deaths."

"They were killed!" She jumped to her feet. "I have to pack."

"Where are you going? We need to be able to contact you."

She rattled off her phone number. "I'm going to Misty Hollow." The last place she'd heard Colt was. She'd read an article online about a new ranch and had seen him in the background of a photo. Hopefully, he would still be there. Hopefully, he wouldn't turn her away. A whole lot of hopefullys for a man she'd walked away from.

Leaving the officer to see himself out, Parker rushed to her room and tossed clothes, toiletries, and anything else she might need into a suitcase. She'd have to withdraw money from an ATM. Misty Hollow would have a bank where she could access more funds. Her mind whirled as she formed an escape plan.

Until she could find out why her parents were killed and why she was now being targeted, she had to leave. She pulled on a pair of sweatpants over her shorts and hurried back to the living room. The officer turned from the window. "You're still here."

He lifted a shoulder. "The scene is being processed. I'm watching to see whether the suspect makes another appearance."

She edged next to him and glanced out the

window. Several people from the apartment complex milled around at the edge of the parking lot. None of them looked like the shadowy figure she'd seen. "I don't see him."

"Maybe this isn't about you at all, Miss Wells."

"I saw the note," she ground out through her teeth. Why wouldn't he believe her about this? Why wouldn't the authorities believe her about her parents' death not being an accident? "Enough. I'm leaving. Call me if you need me." She grabbed her suitcase and purse, then stormed out of the apartment.

Feeling safe with several police officers around, she took the time to put the GPS coordinates to Misty Hollow into her phone before leaving the parking lot and heading north. Maybe she should have thought things through before heading to Misty Hollow. She had to hold onto the hope that Colt would forgive her and help her. Who else could she trust other than the strong, silent, cowboy?

Parker made a quick stop at the bank and withdrew her limit of four-hundred dollars, then stopped to fill up with gas and buy a large coffee. By the time she reached the interstate, her nerves were on edge, and she kept choking back sobs at the image of her friend. Whatever that man had against Parker and her parents had nothing to do with Tanya. How could it?

Now, Parker was on the run with waves of grief washing over her and heading to ask the man whose heart she'd broken to help her. She shook her head, glancing through the rearview mirror. What had happened to her life? How had she gone from the pampered daughter of well-off parents to a scared rabbit on the run? Parker sniffed and swiped a quick hand across her swollen eyes. She didn't have time to cry. Not yet.

The sun peeked over the horizon as she drove through the valley that held Misty Hollow in its palm, then up the mountain toward the Rocking W Ranch. At least that's the directions the man at the last gas station told her.

Misty Hollow lay quiet in the early morning hours. Very few cars cruised the streets. No one walked the sidewalks as the streetlights blinked off. Quiet and calm welcomed her. Thick foliage rose on both sides of the road heading up the mountain. A wall on her left, a cliff on her right, and hairpin turns that kept her speed at a minimum. Since it didn't appear as if anyone had followed her, some of the urgency fell from her shoulders, and Parker allowed herself to enjoy the scenery. Occasionally, she'd glimpse a view of the hollow below, the rising sun kissing the tops of buildings and trees. It wasn't hard to see the allure of such a place. A place where Colt would fit right in.

Her heart stung at how she'd let him go—the pain in his eyes, the white line around his lips as he bit back a retort after she told him her parents would never accept him as a suitable husband. She'd chosen money and position in society over the love of a good man and had regretted it every day since. Would he even listen to her? Give her a chance to explain? He'd probably turn his back on her. She'd spotted a motel on the outskirts of town. If he did send her away, then at least she could go there until she figured out her next step.

The road evened out when she reached the top of the mountain. She parked on the side of the road and got out of the car to admire the view. The town below looked like something out of a postcard as the sun swept away the lingering mist. What splendor it must be in the fall.

Knowing she couldn't stall facing Colt any longer, she climbed back in her car, glanced at her GPS, and headed for the Rocking W.

A wooden, rectangular arch greeted visitors. At the end of a long drive flanked by white fences where horses grazed stood a large three-story house. Behind and to the sides were multiple outbuildings. The picturesque ranch looked well-kept and profitable. She parked in a small parking lot a few yards away from the house and stepped out of the car on trembling legs.

She climbed the steps and raised her hand to knock. The door opened before she could, and a woman in a frilly yellow apron greeted her. Parker forced a smile. "I'm here to speak to Colt Dawson."

"Ranch business or personal? He's our foreman, so we get both kinds." The woman smiled.

"Personal."

"It's early, so he's either in the bunkhouse—she motioned to a sprawling white building—or the barn. Breakfast isn't for another half an hour, so he should be easy to locate."

"Thank you." She returned the woman's smile and headed first for the bunkhouse where a thin, older man by the name of Willy pointed her to the barn.

"Boss is on his honeymoon, so Colt is picking up the slack," he said. "Our barn burned down not too long ago, so he's in that big tin shed for now."

Parker nodded as if she understood and headed for a building that looked nothing like a barn. The metal shed was big and ugly, but the nickers of horses greeted her as she stepped into the dim recess.

She recognized him before he turned around. Faded jeans that fit him just right. A flannel shirt with sleeves rolled up to reveal muscled, tanned forearms. A cowboy hat hanging on a nearby hook. Sand-colored hair tousled from having worn the hat. Hazel eyes that widened at the sight of her.

"Hello, Colt."

~

"Parker?" What in the world was she doing on the Rocking W? Parker Wells was the last person Colt ever expected to see again.

He leaned the shovel he'd been using to clean manure from the stalls and grabbed a wet rag from a nearby bucket to clean his hands. Colt needed a moment to compose himself before moving closer. Not that he needed to—when he straightened, she'd moved close enough he could smell the remnants of a floral perfume.

"I need your help."

The words fell like boulders to the packed dirt floor of the temporary barn. He cleared his throat and tossed the rag back into the bucket. "Mommy and Daddy not helping?"

She paled. "They died right after…you left."

His breath caught, wishing he could take back his words. She didn't deserve them. "I'm sorry for your loss." He really was, despite the cliché. "What happened?"

"Someone killed them, and now that person is after me. I have no one else to turn to."

Well, he hadn't expected those words to come from her mouth. His heart hitched as he studied the fear in her sky-blue eyes. He kicked a three-legged stool closer to her. "Sit. I'm listening."

He didn't speak while she told him of her suspicions that her parents' car had been tampered with, thus causing the accident, what had transpired at the club, then the death of her friend and the threatening note. It all sounded far-fetched to him, and no one knew better than he did that spoiled, little Parker Wells tended to exaggerate. "What do the authorities say?"

Her shoulders slumped. "That there's no proof that my parents' death was anything other than an accident, and there was no note. Do you believe me?" Her gaze locked on his with desperation.

No. He sighed. "It's all…a lot."

She lunged to her feet. "You don't. Sorry to bother you." She stormed to the door.

"Wait." He grabbed her arm, then released her as if it burned. Touching Parker dug up feelings best left buried. "I didn't say that I didn't. I…uh…need time to process."

"You do that." She glared. "While you spend time in your thoughts, I'll be at the motel in town trying not to die." She bolted from the barn with him on her heels.

"Parker, wait."

She whirled to face him, looking like a very angry cat. Her eyes narrowed. "I was a fool to think I could ask you for help. You won't have to see or speak to me again." Tears filled her eyes, and her hand trembled as she swiped her cheek. "I thought you could let bygones be bygones and help the woman you once loved."

Still loved, if he were honest with himself. "I will help you, if there's a need."

"Ugh!" Parker whipped around and stomped

toward her car, the same Mercedes she'd driven while they dated. She slid into the driver's seat and slammed the door. Gravel scattered as she sped away from the ranch, leaving him staring after her.

"What was that all about?" Mrs. White stepped onto the porch.

"An old friend asking for help."

Mrs. White posted a hand on her hip. "Which you didn't give."

"No."

"Why not?"

He faced her. "I don't know if there's a need. Parker has always been…flighty, spoiled…" Beautiful, often sweet and caring—everything he thought he wanted in a woman. How wrong he'd been.

Her eyes narrowed. "There's history there."

"Yes."

"Which means, you should've helped her, whether you thought she needed it or not." She waved a wooden spoon at him. "If she's frightened enough to hunt you down, then she believes there's a threat, even if she's the only one who believes there is. You might be the very person to help her see there isn't."

He cocked his head to the side. "What makes you so wise?"

"I've had my share of troubles, Colt, so I recognize the signs. Mark my words, that girl needs you. If not you, then some other cowboy on a white horse."

But…did he need her in his life again?

Chapter Three

Parker held the tears at bay until after she received her key card and made it to her motel room. Why had she been so stupid as to think Colton would help her? She'd been horrible to him. Petty and spoiled, pushing what she wanted because Mommy and Daddy threatened to withhold her inheritance. Now, they were dead, and she'd lost six months of life with Colt.

She locked the door, then fell back onto the bed, arms splayed, and let the tears fall, soaking her hair and the pillow under her head. She'd allow herself to have a good cry, then she'd lift her chin up and come up with a plan B. Being a smart woman, she'd figure out how to stay alive, find whoever murdered her parents, and bring them to justice.

Swiping her forearm across her eyes, she sniffed and sat up. No more time for sniveling.

She stared at the large suitcase sitting next to the door. What was the sense in unpacking? She'd get a good night's rest, then head back to Little Rock and forget all about Colt and his unforgiving heart.

Disrobing, she headed for the bathroom and turned the shower as hot as she could stand. Once it reached the desired temperature, she stepped under the spray, cried some more, then washed with the free toiletries provided before wrapping a towel around her and climbing into bed.

Surprisingly enough, she fell asleep almost instantly. Her stomach's grumble woke her up. Remembering she'd seen a diner on her way into town, she got dressed, locked the room behind her, and decided to walk the couple of blocks. Since she didn't plan on leaving until morning, it wouldn't hurt to do a little sightseeing of the town that looked like a Norman Rockwell painting.

A bell jingled over the door as she entered Lucy's. Heads turned as a young girl led her to a table near the window.

"First time here?" She asked, handing Parker a menu.

"Yes. What do you recommend?" Parker skimmed the menu, noting homestyle cooking.

"Our chef is a four-star chef from the big city, and everything is good. Today's special is chicken fried steak, mashed potatoes, white gravy, and fried okra."

Not the fine dining she was used to, but it sounded delicious. "I'll have that and a diet soda."

"Be right up." The server took the menu and headed for the kitchen.

A few seconds later, she brought the soda with another promise that the food wouldn't be long. Parker thanked her and stared out the window while she sipped her drink.

A few cars cruised by. Shoppers strolled in and out of stores. The place really did look like a Hallmark movie. It was probably almost magical when it snowed. Maybe she could rent a house and stay for a while.

With internet, she could do a lot of investigating into her parents' death, and Little Rock was only four hours away if she needed to head there to do some snooping. A small town in the middle of the Arkansas Ozarks had to be a safer place to hide out than a much larger city.

After eating a meal that was sure to put five pounds on her hips, she paid the bill in cash and stepped into dusk. Old-fashioned streetlights flickered to life. Parker turned right and strolled past Victorian homes and bungalows with wraparound porches. Beautiful.

People nodded and smiled, and some said hello as they passed. One little girl in particular handed Parker a wilted flower.

"Thank you." Parker turned to watch her walk away with her mother.

Her smile faded and a frown formed as a man ducked into the drugstore. Something about him looked familiar.

She stepped up her pace, crossing at the end of the street. When she passed the drugstore, she glanced inside but didn't see the man. She chuckled, realizing how silly she was, thinking the man who had killed Tanya could have followed her to Misty Hollow. With no connections to the town other than Colt, how could the man follow her here?

Parker did a little window shopping and ducked into a bookstore for something to read before falling asleep in a few hours. She purchased a new rom-com release, a pretty notebook, and a pen to jot down notes for her investigation, then pushed the door open and stepped outside.

There he stood. The same man who had ducked into the drugstore was watching her from across the street. He stood under a streetlamp, hat pulled low, looking exactly like the man she'd spotted outside her apartment. So, he had followed her—the man who had slit her friend's throat and written that note.

Her heart leaped into her throat, and she picked up her pace. Was he following her? She didn't dare look back, but she'd have to ditch him before heading back to the motel.

She ducked back into Lucy's and headed for the ladies' restroom. Noticing the exit door at the end of the hallway, she passed the restroom and stepped outside into an alley. Now, she ran in the direction of the motel.

Inside her room, she locked the door, pulled the curtains tight, and called the front desk. "I need the number to the Rocking W Ranch, please."

"I don't have that number."

"Can you get it for me?"

The manager sighed. "Okay, but you could look it up as easy as I can."

Parker widened her eyes. How spoiled was she? "You're right. Sorry to have bothered you." She sat on the bed and pulled up the needed information on her phone, then called the ranch and asked for Colton Dawson.

~

"This is Colt Dawson."

"A man is following me."

"Parker?"

"Yes, I know you don't want to hear from me, but I don't know what to do." Her words broke on a sob. "I think I lost him, but I'm not sure. No! He's outside the motel, Colt."

He was already reaching for his hat and gun.

"What does he look like?"

"I can't see his face, but about your height, maybe twenty pounds heavier, dark clothes, dark hat pulled low over his face. A baseball cap. There's an emblem, but I can't read it."

"What's he doing?"

"Staring at my window."

"Stay in your room. I'll be there in twenty minutes."

"That long?"

"I'll be flying as it is." He hung up and turned to Mrs. White. "Looks like we'll be having a guest."

"I'll put the coffee on." She reached into the cabinet.

Colt ran for his truck. The obvious fear in her voice had him tearing down the mountain faster than was safe. He couldn't help her if he was dead, so he slowed down.

He'd done his best to forget about her—to heal his broken heart. If this was a ploy to get him in her clutches again, he'd strangle her himself. Colt didn't want her to be in danger, but he couldn't stand lying, and, if Parker was anything, she was an occasional liar. Nothing big, just little things to get what she wanted. It was her parents' fault for spoiling her, but as a woman of twenty-five, she was responsible for her own actions now. He'd help her, but he wouldn't trust her.

As he neared the motel, he slowed the truck and scanned both sides of the street. Not seeing anyone, he parked in front of the building and dialed Parker. "Which room are you in?"

"103."

He closed his eyes and exhaled. Didn't she know a

single woman shouldn't take a ground-floor room in motels where the doors all faced the outside? "I'm here. Stay there." Colt shoved his door open and marched to room 103. He knocked and waited as she peered out the window before opening the door.

"Thank you." She threw her arms around her neck. "I've never been more terrified in my life."

He unwound her arms from him. "That your suitcase?"

"Yes."

He grabbed it and carried it to his truck where he tossed it in the back. "You can stay at the ranch tonight. Tomorrow, we'll discuss the next step."

"The next step is me proving my parents were murdered."

He took a deep breath and counted to ten before opening the passenger side door for her. "We'll discuss it in the morning."

"Do you think I can stay at the ranch while I investigate?" She climbed onto the seat.

"No one stays at the ranch without working for their keep." He slammed the door. The last thing he wanted was for her to live there. Even one night was too long.

"I'm sure there's a job I can do," she said once he sat in the driver's seat.

"Like what?" He frowned. "You've never worked a day in your life."

"I'm sure there's something." She put a hand on his arm, her nails professionally manicured and sporting a light pink shade of polish. "Thank you, Colt." She turned to face out the window.

"Let me know if you see the guy." If someone

really was following Parker with the intent to harm her, then they'd need to pay a visit to the sheriff. That, too, could wait until tomorrow. He'd add taking Parker to the sheriff's office to his long to-do list. Right after interviewing a construction company about rebuilding the barn.

Thankfully, Parker didn't talk until they reached the ranch. The moment he stopped, she shoved open her door without waiting for him and struggled to drag her suitcase from the truck bed.

Colt easily lifted it out and carried it to the house. "Mrs. White, meet Parker Wells."

"Nice to meet you, dear. Come have a cup of coffee, then I'll show you to your room."

Knowing Parker was now in good hands, Colt excused himself and marched to the office of his boss, Dylan Wyatt. Helping a damsel in distress or not, he had work to do, and with Dylan on his honeymoon, both the boss and the foreman jobs fell on Colt's shoulders.

The leather chair creaked as he lowered himself into it. He picked up a pen and tapped it on the desk blotter. What job could he give Parker, and how much could the ranch afford to pay her?

The day camps during the summer and the camping tours had put the ranch back into the black— that and the insurance money from the barn burning. Parker had absolutely no experience with cooking or children that he knew of. Maybe Mrs. White needed help readying the guest rooms for the survival-training classes that took place over the weekends, and for those who wanted to experience a bit of ranch life for a day or two. Parker could stay in one of the newly-built staff cottages that were slowly replacing the bunkhouse, since several of the ranch hands had expressed the desire to marry someday.

Fools. Didn't they know that love only brought pain?

He'd been surprised to see Dylan marry. His first wife had died falling from a horse, then the new one had almost been killed by a madman.

Now, another woman set foot on the ranch with an alleged killer dogging her steps. Colt removed his hat and tossed it on a chair across from him. If he wanted to get to bed, he needed to finish the payroll. He didn't have time for what-ifs. He'd dig deeper into the potential danger following Parker in the morning.

Staring out the window, he prayed danger wouldn't come to the ranch. He also prayed for wisdom to make the right decisions that would save those living there.

Chapter Four

After a fitful night of shadowy figures looming over her bed, Parker shuffled downstairs in hopes of a cup of coffee. Mrs. White and another woman, Marilyn Cooper, if she remembered correctly, bustled around the kitchen.

"Good morning." Mrs. White thrust a cup of coffee into her hands. "Colt is already out and hard at work. He said if you're staying more than a day, we're to put you to work. Are you?"

"Staying more than a day?" Parker blinked at the cup in her hand. Never a morning person, being bombarded with questions first thing didn't register well with her. "Most likely, yes." What kind of work? She could ride a horse but had never saddled or curried one.

"How about housecleaning before and after guests?" The aproned cook pointed toward a chair at the table. "Sit. Breakfast was served half an hour ago, but we saved you a plate." She set a plate of biscuits and chocolate gravy on the table. "Something to pick you up a bit."

"I love chocolate gravy." Parker sat and picked up her knife and fork.

"Good, but don't get used to the special treatment. Starting tomorrow, be down at six for breakfast, or you don't eat. And you'll have to eat what everyone else does." She patted Parker on the shoulder. "But, since today is your first day, and you've had a hard time of it, we made an exception."

"Thank you." She stared at her plate for a minute, then dug in. She'd ignore the calories for now. A girl running from a madman needed sustenance. "Can I get the Wi-Fi password, please? And what are my hours, day off…?"

Mrs. White wiped her hands with a dishtowel. "The password is on the side of the fridge. You'll only work on days we have guests coming and going, and you'll be moving into a cottage out back. All the staff now have their own little houses, courtesy of Mr. Wyatt."

"How long has he been gone?" Wasn't he on his honeymoon?

"A couple of months. He'll be back when he's ready. The ranch is in capable hands with Colt running things." She filled the sink with hot water while Marilyn cleared the table, sending Parker sideways glances. "He's looking for horse-breeding stock in Europe."

Her eyes lit up. "I can give him some contact numbers." Her father had loved betting on the horse races and knew people in high places. Parker bit into buttery, chocolatey goodness and closed her eyes in bliss. She could almost forget about her trouble eating the wonderful gravy and flaky biscuits.

Add an action tag. "Great. Give Colt the info and he'll email Dylan." She plunged her hands into a sink full of sudsy water. "Your cottage is number three. Feel free to move in when you've finished your breakfast."

She sipped her coffee while listening to the whispered conversation between the two other women. Occasionally, she'd hear the word, *trouble*, and, *the sheriff won't be happy*. Enough to know they were talking about her.

When she finished, she handed her plate to Mrs. White, who held up a palm. "Scrape it into the bin, then place it in the sink."

Right. Parker had a lot to learn about not having servants. Even in her apartment, she had a woman come in once a day to tidy up. Which reminded her that she needed to call Molly and let her know her services weren't needed for the time being.

Parker put her plate in the sink, then went back to her room to pack the few items she'd pulled from her suitcase the night before. Dragging her bag behind her, she thumped down the back stairs to search for cottage number three.

Several men in cowboy hats spared her a glance before returning to their work. A horse nickered; a dog barked. To her left lay a pile of burned lumber large enough to have been a building. Just past that was a long rectangular building, the bunkhouse where she'd looked for Colt. She turned to the right. There stood five tiny houses cute and small enough to grace a postcard.

Number three was yellow with blue shutters. The door opened easily at her touch, revealing a living area, a galley-style kitchen, and a small bathroom. A set of stairs with drawers built into them led to a sleeping loft. Tiny but perfect for one person. Especially one who hoped to stay a short time only. Just until she could solve her parents' murder and put the killer behind bars.

"Hope it's sufficient."

She shrieked and whipped around to see Colt standing in the doorway. "You scared me."

"Sorry. You're the first person to live in this one. Let me know if there's anything you need. We can stop and pick up groceries when we head into town to speak to the sheriff. The cabinets are stocked with dishes and linens. You can do your laundry in the main house." He rattled off the details in a detached voice as he might to a complete stranger.

She sighed. "It's perfect. Sheriff?"

He gave a curt nod. "I thought it wise to let Sheriff Westbrook in on your suspicions about being threatened."

"It's a fact, Colton, not a suspicion. Let me get settled in first, okay?" Just one more person who didn't believe her. Why did his disbelief hurt so much more than everyone else's? "Where can I find you?"

He headed to the door. "I'll be in the temporary barn. Make sure you have a list for groceries. I don't have a lot of time to waste."

Surly attitude. She headed up the stairs as his footsteps retreated.

A queen-sized bed covered by what looked like a handmade quilt provided color to the loft. Two small closets stood on each side. A dresser formed a half wall between the loft and the downstairs. The whole place was adorable.

She put her clothes away, stacked the books she'd recently purchased on the dresser, and surveyed the few things she'd brought with her. Nothing compared to what remained in her apartment, yet she felt…lighter somehow.

Once the killer was caught, it might be time for Parker to reassess her priorities.

~

After he took Parker to see the sheriff, if he could just stay busy, he might not have to see much of her. But what if the sheriff believed her? What if Colt was asked to watch over her? The last thing he wanted was to be the babysitter to the woman who had cast him off because he wasn't good enough to be her husband.

"I'm ready."

He turned. Parker stood just outside the door, the sun highlighting her walnut-colored hair. Her blue eyes remained hidden in the shadows. Always the epitome of fashion, Parker wore skinny jeans and a pink frilly blouse.

Despite his pain, he couldn't help but remember the scent of her hair as he held her in his arms. Something floral and expensive. She'd barely had to tilt her face when he'd kissed her, her five-foot-nine inches fitting perfectly against his six-foot-two.

He gave an inward groan—this wasn't going to be easy. "Let me wash up." He marched past her, angry at the path his thoughts had taken, and washed his hands and forearms at a horse trough set up for that purpose.

"Why don't you wash up in the house?"

He spun around to see her staring at him, a fist posted on her hip. "Mrs. White forbids us to bring anything dirty or foul into the house. Manure is at the top of that list." He dried off with a towel hanging on the branch of a nearby tree.

"Why don't you have one of the other men shovel

the manure?" She frowned, wrinkling her nose.

"There are no servants here, Parker. We all pitch in, which is also expected of you if you plan on staying."

"I am. I will." She jogged to keep up with him as he strode toward his truck.

"We could use some feed, Colt." The older cowboy yelled from the paddock. "What we got is wet."

Colt shook his head. Not having a proper barn caused all kinds of problems he hadn't anticipated. "Send a list of what we need to the co-op. I'll make a stop." He'd have a lot to put in an email to Dylan that evening, starting with Parker.

Since the ranch's mission was to help those in trouble, Dylan would welcome her, but Colt still couldn't help but think it might be a ploy to get his attention. Now that her parents were gone, God rest their souls, Parker might be hoping to reconcile with him. Not a chance. He deserved more than a woman who chose her inheritance over the man she supposedly loved. Nope. He wouldn't put himself in that situation again. If Parker wanted a cowboy, there were other available men on the ranch.

Huffing, Colt opened the truck door for her. Even if he wanted to keep his distance from Parker, his mother would reach down from heaven and box his ears if he didn't act like a gentleman.

"What would you do if you suspected your parents were murdered?" She asked as he pulled away from the ranch. "Not suspected. Knew. You knew they were murdered."

"Okay. Why?" His knuckles whitened as he

gripped the steering wheel. He wasn't in the mood for conversation. "What's the motive?"

"Money. It's always money or revenge." Her eyes widened. "Maybe it's both."

"Again…why? Did they have enemies?"

She shrugged. "Dad didn't talk to me about his business."

"Construction, right?"

"Yes, so why kill him?"

"Exactly."

"You're so infuriating, Colton Dawson." She crossed her arms and flounced back against the seat. "I'm going with my instincts. One of these days, you'll see I'm right, and you'll apologize."

Not likely. "Why not ask LRPD to help you?"

"They don't believe me," she said softly. "Just like everyone else. No evidence doesn't mean a crime wasn't committed. They could at least look into things."

He fought the urge to shake his head. "I'm sure they did."

"I'm not talking to you anymore." She lifted her chin and stared out the window.

He grinned, having gotten what he wanted—a quiet ride into town.

"Why Misty Hollow?"

He should've known she couldn't go long without talking. "Why not?"

AT "It's…secluded."

"Which is why I like it."

"It does have charm, I'll admit. I'm thinking about relocating."

God forbid. "There's no nightlife here, Parker."

"That no longer interests me." She shot him a

frigid glance. "A lot has happened in six months to make me see things differently." Her gaze softened. "I'm sorry, Colton. I really am." She turned her attention back outside.

He didn't know what to make of her apology. Did it mean anything to him? Maybe she was lying. Only time would tell. Did he *want* to accept her apology? No. Would he? Yes, because it was the right thing to do, even if it put him at risk of further pain. Colt wasn't too worried about her staying in Misty Hollow. She'd grow bored soon enough, and he'd be free of her again. He'd have to harden his heart all over and push any thoughts of Parker Wells deep inside to keep the hurt at bay.

"What kind of man is the sheriff?"

AT "A fair one. Former FBI. This town has seen more than its share of trouble, but it's always come out on the other side in fair-enough shape." He'd grown to love the place despite the trouble over the last year. Now, he cast a sideways glance at her. Trouble might have once again arrived in Misty Hollow. Last time, one of the ranch hands had been killed. Hopefully, this time, no one would die. *If* Parker was telling the truth, and that was a great big if.

Chapter Five

Parker told herself she no longer cared whether people believed she was being stalked or not. She did, though; in fact, she cared very much, but she wouldn't let their disbelief sway her.

She released a pent-up breath and climbed into the passenger seat of Colt's truck before he could open the door for her. They worked together, nothing more. *Work.* She'd never had a job in her life. "Colt, I also need to stop by the bank, please. I need to transfer my account since I'll be here for a while."

A muscle ticked in his jaw, the only sign he wasn't excited about her sticking around. Rather than say anything, he nodded.

They stopped at the bank first. Colt stayed in the vehicle while Parker went inside. The bank manager, Wilson Stephens, seemed overjoyed to have an account the size of hers transferred to his bank.

"I'm not sure how long I'll be staying, but I'm living and working at the Rocking W for now." She smiled and took the account book he offered her before returning to the truck.

Before climbing inside, she glanced up and down the sidewalk. No one seemed to pay her any undue attention. Shoppers strolled, cars passed, folks went in and out of the diner on a regular basis. Some of the tension in her shoulders slipped away. She was safe in this picturesque town of Misty Hollow.

"If it's fine with you, we'll park at the co-op, then walk to the sheriff's office and market."

Not a question really. "That's fine." She doubted the sheriff would believe her either. Seeing him would be nothing but a waste of time.

After a short walk from the co-op, Parker found herself seated across from a handsome man with shrewd eyes and a faint five o'clock shadow who studied her for a long moment before speaking. He shot Colt a quick glance, then said, "What can I do for you? I'm assuming there's trouble at the ranch?"

"Not yet." Colt shrugged. "This is Parker Wells. She's…working there for a while and believes she's being stalked by a man who killed her parents."

The sheriff's brows rose. "I'm listening."

Parker told him of her suspicions regarding her parents' death, the man at the bar, the murder of Tanya, and the note that disappeared. When she'd finished, she crossed her arms and waited for him to dismiss her.

Sheriff Westbrook leaned back in his chair, his sharp gaze focused on her. "You're positive?"

"Absolutely." Did he believe her? "Why would I make this up?"

"I'll look up the report on your parents' accident, but it's the murder of your friend that concerns me. That can't be ruled as an accident. Note or no note, I believe you might be in danger because of the fact her body was discovered outside your apartment." He mumbled something about a new woman to town always bringing trouble.

"What do I do now?"

AT "Stay vigilant. It's highly unlikely the man followed you here, but he could have without you noticing. Unless you're trained in surveillance?"

She shook her head. Tears burned her eyes. Finally, someone believed her. At least part of her story. "Will you let me know what you think after reading the report on my parents?"

"Yes." He glanced at Colt. "Since the two of you are both living and working at the ranch, keep an eye on her, okay? Let me know if anything suspicious happens."

Colt's face darkened, and his shoulders slumped. "I can do that."

"Not if it's going to hurt that much." Parker glared.

The sheriff's eyes darted from him to her and back. "You two have a history?"

"Nothing I can't handle." Colt bolted up and offered the sheriff his hand in a shake. "Thank you, sir." With a nod at Parker, he motioned for her to exit the office ahead of him.

Head high, she marched outside, then whirled to face him. "That was embarrassing."

"What was?" He frowned.

"Your obvious distaste of keeping an eye on me. Don't bother, Colton. I can take care of myself. Which way is the grocery store?"

"Two blocks toward the co-op, then turn right." He fell into step beside her. "Give me time, Parker. You show up on my doorstep after six months, reinsert yourself into my life, and bring trouble with you. It's a lot."

"I figured a big strong cowboy like you could handle something like this. You were in the Marines, Colton. You've seen a lot more danger than I could ever bring." Her eyes shimmered. "If I had anyone else to ask for help, I would, believe me."

A pained look crossed his face. "None of your high-society friends were willing?"

She stopped, hands on her hips, and stared up at him. How could he be so dense? "Whoever is after me would know about those friends, now, wouldn't he?"

AT "They would also know about me."

True, but Colt had what it took to keep her safe. "You're impossible." She stormed past him down the sidewalk, turning right after two blocks.

His voice rang out behind her. "I'll bring the truck and meet you in the store."

Whatever.

A blast of cool air hit her in the face as she stepped inside the store and grabbed a cart. She headed for the produce, filling the cart with fruit and vegetables.

Colt chuckled when he caught up to her. "You still eat mostly rabbit food?"

"I happen to like fresh produce, although I do eat fish, chicken, and the occasional steak." She headed for the butcher next. She didn't need much since she lived alone, and her cooking skills weren't even close to being chef-like, but she'd manage.

~

Mark Collins widened his eyes at the sight of Parker perusing the fish in the butcher case. He'd followed her to Misty Hollow but hadn't expected her to be out and about so soon after the death of her friend.

His gaze shifted to the man next to her. A cowboy

over six-feet tall, muscles straining the tee-shirt he wore, and a scowl that dared anyone to get close. So, she'd found herself a bodyguard. It wouldn't do any good.

Her family had ruined him, and he would get his revenge on their daughter. Pulling his baseball cap low over his eyes, he headed in the opposite direction before he attracted the cowboy's attention.

A bulletin board with homemade help-wanted ads brought a grin. Looked like the Rocking W Ranch needed construction workers. The phone number to a local construction company sat under the notice. Mark jotted it down on the back of a receipt from his pocket. This would put him right under Parker's nose, and she wouldn't suspect a thing. Then, when the time was right and he had her frightened enough, he'd take her. She'd beg for death by the time he finished with her.

~

Colt carried Parker's purchases outside and put them in the trunk. He'd noticed the man watching her in the butcher section of the store, but a woman with her looks, dressed in clothes worth a regular person's weekly wage, merited a second glance. When he spotted the man outside the store, he thought there might be more to his attention.

His eyes narrowed as the man darted across the street and ducked into the mercantile.

Colt stashed the groceries in the truck before leading Parker into the co-op. He wouldn't grow too suspicious unless he saw the man again.

"Howdy, Colt. Willy called in the order, and it's waiting out back for you." The owner, Henry strained against the denim overalls he wore. "Do you need anything else?

"I need a new tool to shave the mule's hooves, a couple of shovels—" he rattled off items destroyed in the barn fire. "Send the bill to the ranch, okay?"

Henry nodded, glancing to where Parker browsed the shelves of cowboy boots and hats. "She yours?"

"Hardly. She's a new employee. Parker will be helping Mrs. White with the rooms."

"Hmm. Doesn't look the type."

Parker set a pair of pink cowboy boots on the counter. "I'll take these. Do you have a hat to match?"

Henry's eyes widened. "Yes, ma'am. What about jeans? You'll need some sturdy ones if you're working at the ranch. Women's duds are over there." He jerked his thumb toward the back of the store.

"Do we have time?" She asked Colt.

He nodded, eying the hat Henry set next to the boots. *Pink*? He shook his head.

Parker returned with a plaid pink top with fringe, another one with pearl buttons, and two pairs of sturdy jeans. The jeans were the only sensible items, in Colt's opinion. Parker whipped out a credit card. "You do take credit, right?"

"Yes, ma'am." Henry shook his head and rang up the items. "That it?"

"That's it." She grinned and hefted the bags he'd set on the counter.

Colt took them from her. "We'll drive around back to pick up the things for the ranch."

AT "I'm a cowgirl now."

"Clothes do not a cowgirl make." He set the bags with the groceries.

"I can ride as well as you, and now I'll look the

part."

"Okay." He wanted to quote her Gene Autry's Cowboy's Creed, but wisely kept his mouth shut, reciting it to himself.

Gene Autry's Cowboy Code of Honor

1. A cowboy never takes unfair advantage—even of an enemy.
2. A cowboy never betrays a trust. He never goes back on his word.
3. A cowboy always tells the truth.
4. A cowboy is kind and gentle to small children, old folks, and animals.
5. A cowboy is free from racial and religious intolerance.
6. A cowboy is always helpful when someone is in trouble.
7. A cowboy is always a good worker.
8. A cowboy respects women, his parents, and his nation's laws.
9. A cowboy is clean about his person in thought, word, and deed.
10. A cowboy is a patriot.

Parker had a few of the cowboy qualities, but like Colt, she had a whole lot of work to do in other areas. Working on a ranch didn't make anyone a cowboy or a cowgirl. He considered himself a ranch hand. To be a cowboy of Gene Autry's standards at least, he'd need to be almost perfect.

A man stood in the back of the co-op ready to help

load the feed and other items into the bed of the truck. He shot Parker a quick look, his gaze lingering longer than Colt liked.

Colt cleared his throat.

The guy jerked to attention and resumed loading. "Ain't seen her around here before."

"That would be because she hasn't been here more than a day." He crossed his arms and glared, not sure if the man's attention or Colt's reaction to that attention rankled more. Colt no longer had any claim on Parker Wells, and he preferred it that way.

Movement across the lot drew his attention. The same man he'd spotted in the grocery store entered the diner. It shouldn't be suspicious, but something about him set off alarms in Colt. The furtive way he kept his face averted. The hunched shoulders as if he didn't want to be seen. The man warranted watching for sure.

Parker glanced up from her phone when Colt climbed into the driver's seat. "Everything good?"

"Yep." He threw the truck into drive and pulled away from the building. "Anything else before we head back up the mountain?"

"I could use some more books. I like to read in the evening and only have two."

How many books could a person read? "That's going to take a while, ain't it?"

She laughed. "I'll order them online and have them delivered. Head to the ranch."

He breathed a sigh of relief and headed up the mountain. Weekends were always busy, and the upcoming one would be no different. A group of businessmen wanted to experience a couple of nights in the "wild" as a corporate-bonding activity, and it was up to Colt to make sure it happened.

Parker chattered on about her new clothes.

Colt listened with half an ear, his mind on the myriad of other things he still had left to do before heading to bed that night. Not to mention the lingering unease about the man who'd been tracking them.

Chapter Six

Colt bolted upright, the sheets under him soaked with perspiration. He rubbed his hands roughly over his face to wipe away the images from the nightmare that visited him far too regularly.

A glance at the clock sent him flopping back onto his pillow. Three a.m. after a long night. He groaned and rested his forearm across his eyes.

Facing the realization that Parker was in real trouble and not just trying to get attention brought back the horrors of his brief tour in the Middle East. His team had stormed a compound, guns blazing. Women and children had been caught in the fire.

One woman in particular had torn at his heart. She'd reached out, imploring him to take her hand. He'd gripped it as the last light left her eyes. He hadn't been able to save her or any of the others. What if he couldn't save Parker? How could he keep his distance from the woman if he had to protect her? Life had become very complicated.

Sleep refused to come despite lying there for another hour. He sat up, stretched, then made his way to the shower. As foreman of the ranch, he'd been the first to get a tiny house of his own. His large frame barely fit in the shower framed with a metal lip and a curtain that wrapped two-thirds around the opening.

The hot water washed the sweat from his body and the terrors of his nightmare down the drain—at least for a while. Colt made himself a cup of coffee and carried it onto the postage-stamp porch of his house. The sun peeked over the horizon, kissing clouds with orange and crimson.

Someday, he'd own his own ranch, then he'd marry and have a family. In that order. Maybe not here on Misty Mountain, but there were other places to raise cattle. He'd leave the horse-ranching to Dylan.

Lights flickered on in house number three. He couldn't remember Parker ever getting up before nine. Maybe her brain was on overdrive, the same as his. She had lost both her parents and him in six months' time. Now an alleged killer stalked her. Those were plenty of reasons for sleep to flee.

Cup in hand, she stepped onto her porch wearing an oversized shirt and shorts, looking way too adorable for a man trying very hard to keep his distance. Seeing him, she raised a hand in greeting, then returned inside her house. She might be up early, but she was no more a morning person than she was six months ago.

He chuckled and finished his coffee as the ranch came to life. When the ranch hands started filtering from the bunkhouse, he went inside to put on a shirt before heading to the main house for breakfast. At nine, he'd start interviewing construction workers.

Since the trouble a few months ago, Dylan insisted that all workers hired by the construction crew be interviewed and given a background check. It had slowed down progress, but Colt would finish up with the interviews that day, and building could start tomorrow. Hopefully, there would be a barn when the boss and his family returned from Europe.

He filed into the dining room with the others and took his seat seconds before Parker shuffled in. She'd pulled her hair back into a ponytail, wore no makeup, and her clothes looked as if she'd slept in them. It didn't stop the men from eyeing her, though. It would take a lot more than an early-morning mussing to make Parker unattractive.

Fighting the urge to glare at the other ranch hands, he reached for the tray of biscuits and put four on his plate before ladling a healthy serving of white country-sausage gravy over the pile.

Parker paled. "That's a lot of food, Colt."

"Yeah?" He arched a brow.

"I mean…how can you eat all that?"

"Healthy appetite and working hard." He scooped a big bite into his mouth. Why single him out? The other men ate just as much.

She put half a biscuit on her plate and added a scant amount of gravy.

Colt shook his head. His stomach would think his throat had been cut if he ate no more than that.

When he'd finished, he excused himself, asked Mrs. White to send any interviewees to the office, and headed that way.

"I'm busy. Parker will have to escort them," the older woman said loud enough for him to hear. "Right after she makes herself presentable."

He chuckled and sat at the desk to respond to emails until the first appointment. Parker could never be unpresentable once she shook off the aftereffects of sleep.

At three minutes past nine, Parker brought the owner of the construction company into his office. The man thrust out his hand. "David Townsend of Townsend Construction. We're happy for your business. Why the need for interviews of my workers?"

Colt returned the man's handshake, then motioned for him to have a seat. "Mr. Wyatt's request."

"Okay, but no need to do background checks. Save yourself the time. My company does them before we hire anyone."

"Have you received them all back?"

"Except for a few. The last few should be in any day now. If something looks off, the man will be fired on the spot."

Colt nodded. The results of Townsend's vetting would come back before any Colt requested. "Your company come highly recommended."

"I sure hope so." The man grinned. "My competitor ended up being a cold-blooded killer. No one else has arrived to take any business from me. Misty Hollow would be up a creek if I didn't run a company they could count on."

"How many men?"

"Twelve. We'll be here at six a.m. and work until three, weather permitting. Do you have the plans so I can make sure I have the supplies by tomorrow?"

Colt handed him rolled-up blueprints. "Have the supplies billed to the ranch unless they were included in the contract."

"Mr. Wyatt approved them in the contract. Nothing for you to worry about."

Great. Colt had enough on his plate.

For the next couple of hours, men came in and out of the revolving door of his office. Colt breathed a sigh of relief when the last man entered.

"Mark Collins. I'm new to Misty Hollow." The man sat across from him. "Couldn't believe my luck in landing a job so soon." He smiled. "Nice ranch."

"Thanks." Colt hoped he worked as much as he liked to talk.

"Those tiny houses out back are cute. They for rent?"

"No, sir, those are for ranch hands only. If you're looking for a place to rent, the realtor in town should know of some rentals. What brought you to Misty Hollow?"

"I used to vacation up this way as a kid. Liked it then and hope I like it as much now. Guess I'll know whether I stay or go after this job is done."

Colt thanked the man for his time and excused him, waiting a few seconds before leaving the office. He didn't want to get caught up in a full-blown conversation with any of the workers who might be wandering around getting a feel for the place.

Sure enough, several of them leaned against the corral and watched as River Swanson, one of the hands, put a yearling through its paces. Let them see it all today, so they'd focus on building the next day.

~

Once the interviews were over, Parker had nothing to do. She took her laptop to the back deck of the main house, set a glass of sweet tea on the table next to a chair, and then settled down to dig into the accident that took the life of her parents.

Parker had read the report before, but there had to

be more. She'd posted several things online herself voicing her beliefs. Eventually, she'd get a clue that would help her. She refused to give up hope.

Her heart had almost stopped that morning when she'd spotted a shirtless Colt two doors down. Then, she'd scurried into her house like a frightened rabbit. Real mature, Parker.

Once her laptop booted up, she went through emails from her query into a private investigator. The man agreed to take the case for fifty bucks an hour. Parker agreed. Finally, some help.

Not that she didn't intend to do some of the footwork herself, because she did, but having the investigator pounding the pavements, too, would only be a good thing. Divide up the work and all that. Parker drummed her fingers on the arm of the deck chair. She needed a full day off to drive to Little Rock and pay another visit to the police department there. They still hadn't given her a copy of the police report from Tanya's death or her parents. Would Sheriff Westbrook get them for her?

As far as she knew, nothing was happening on the ranch that warranted her being there. Except for the construction workers. Would she be expected to do something for them? If not, she could head to Little Rock. Otherwise, maybe next week? Definitely not the weekend. They always had guests Friday and Saturday nights, she'd been told.

Colt rode by on a black horse, a cowboy hat on his head that matched the color of the horse, one hand holding the reins.

Parker's mouth dried, and she reached for her tea, keeping her gaze on Colt. Her hand knocked the glass, sending tea and ice onto her lap, barely missing the laptop on the side table. She shrieked and jumped to her feet.

"Whoa!" Colt reined his horse to a halt and reached for the gun on his hip. "What is it?"

"Oh. I…uh…" She waved at the puddle in her lap. "Spilled my tea."

He glowered. "I thought you saw a snake." Shaking his head, he clicked his tongue for the horse to move on.

Face heated, she gathered the laptop and glass and rushed back to her house to change. Hopefully, Colt didn't know the reason she'd spilt her tea. The man avoided her like she was the snake he thought she'd seen. No way would she force herself on him.

He may have been asked by the sheriff to keep an eye on her, but he could do that from a distance. They lived and worked on the same ranch after all.

Exchanging her leggings for shorts, she stepped back outside, this time with a book in her hand. She sat in the chair on her tiny porch, propped her feet on the railing, and started to read about a serial killer plaguing a small town. Maybe not the best thing to read when someone was out to kill her, but it would hopefully keep her mind off a certain handsome, hazel-eyed cowboy.

~

She'd been right there. So close he could smell the floral cologne she wore. They'd walked side by side to the foreman's office. Slipping a knife between her ribs would've been easy. But, it was too soon. He wanted her to suffer for the humiliation her parents had heaped on his head with their allegations.

What was the big deal if he'd skimmed a few bucks from the company? It wasn't as if they needed the hundred-thousand he'd taken. Then they'd had the audacity to confront him. To tell him that if he didn't leave and never come back, they'd report him to the authorities.

Him—Mark Collins. His family could be traced back to the early 1700s when they'd first settled in the state. How dare they threaten to sully his family name!

If his great-grandfather hadn't gambled away the family fortune, it would've been Mr. and Mrs. Wells working for him. He let his gaze sweep over Parker sitting on her porch, before returning it to the cowboy in the corral. It wouldn't do for anyone to think he paid Parker too much attention.

He had to bide his time and strike when the time was right. The waiting and planning were almost as good as what he'd imagined killing the last of the Wells family would be like.

Chapter Seven

After a few days of not being able to leave the ranch for one reason or another, Parker contacted the manager of the storage complex where her parents used to store outdated files and asked them to hire someone to deliver the boxes to the ranch. Now, she watched two men carry box after box into her tiny house and stack them against the wall.

"Doesn't leave much room, Lady," one of them said.

"I have enough." Other than sleeping, she spent most of her time helping out in the main house. She handed each man a twenty-dollar bill, then turned to study the boxes that reached as high as her head and filled one wall. There had to be over twenty boxes, and these were only for the current year.

She wasn't sure what she'd find, but her father had kept impeccable records. There would be something in those boxes to help her find their killer.

A quick glance at her phone had her scurrying to the main house, locking the door behind her. With Marilyn on a ranch errand, that left Mrs. White without help for the noon meal. Not that Parker could help cook, but she could set the table and fetch ingredients from the pantry. Things a child could do.

"What's happening at your place?" Mrs. White covered a chicken leg with breadcrumbs.

"Files from my father's office. I hope they'll help me find out who killed him." She put on an apron while staring out the kitchen window.

Men scurried around the barn site. Having cleared the debris and marked the foundation, they were ready to pour the cement. The original barn had only had dirt floors.

"When does Mr. Wyatt return?" Parker lifted the stack of plates from the counter.

"No idea. He left the return date open. Take those to the table under the tent. Too many to feed in the kitchen."

"You're feeding more than the ranch hands?"

"Absolutely. If you're here at mealtime, you get fed." She winked. "Plus, Colt told me to cook enough for everyone."

Parker shrugged and carried the first load of plates outside.

"Let me." A man who looked to be around forty years of age reached for the plates. "I'm headed back from the port-a-potty and can take these. I'm Mark Collins."

"Thank you. I'm Parker Wells." She smiled and returned to the house for the rest of the plates. When she returned outside, Mark was waiting for her. Since she was used to a man's attention and had no qualms about having men work for her, she handed him the plates and went inside for utensils.

When she returned outside again, Colt was waiting for her rather than Mark. "I sent him on his way. He isn't being paid to help you."

She grinned. "Jealous?"

His eyes flashed. "What's with all the boxes you had delivered?"

Okay. Not jealous or in a teasing mood. She explained how she hoped to find something of value inside. "I won't stop until the man who killed my parents and Tanya is brought to justice."

"Sticking your nose into police business can get you killed right along with them."

"So be it." She stepped around him and set the utensils on the table with the plates. "I'm going to do this, Colton. You can either help me or stay out of my way."

He made a noise deep in his throat then marched to survey the work around the barn.

Infuriating man. She stomped back to the kitchen. Half an hour later, she helped Mrs. White carry platters heaping with food to the table where the men would serve themselves. Parker filled a plate for herself and carried it into the house. Heaven forbid she should encourage anyone to talk to her instead of finish eating in the short time Colt had allowed for lunch.

At the last minute, she veered toward her house. With at least a half an hour to spare, she could start going through one of the boxes while she ate. She sat cross-legged on the floor and opened the first box. Tax receipts. She quickly scanned through them as she bit into a chicken leg. Crunchy and golden brown on the outside, moist on the inside. Would Mrs. White teach her to cook if she asked? She'd love to know how to do more than make the simplest of dishes.

The tax records told her nothing more than how

much her father was worth and the myriad of deductions he used. One of the sheets listed employees. People who had been laid off shortly after his death.

Parker had hated doing that, but she knew nothing about the construction business. She glanced out her open door to where the men worked. As the pampered daughter of a wealthy man, she'd kept her head in the sand. That was all about to change.

After finishing her lunch and helping Mrs. White clean up after the noon meal, Parker had a few hours before she was needed again. She returned to the boxes. Soon the arca around here was filled with printed emails, receipts, handwritten notes, and a leather journal she'd found wrapped in a newspaper.

Tears filled her eyes as she opened the book and saw her father's handwriting. She hugged the book to her chest, then carried it outside to her chair on the porch, intending to spend the next few hours visiting with her father.

~

Look at her sitting there like a queen reading a book instead of working. Spoiled, pampered princess. Mark swiped his arm across his sweating brow. Just like her father had been. Not bothering to lift a finger or get his hands dirty. The man had morals, he'd said. Well, Mark had shown him just what those morals had been worth.

He jerked his attention back to the job at hand before the foreman caught him watching her again. Mark couldn't afford to be fired. Not yet. Not until he'd accomplished what he'd come for. Before he killed her, he'd have her transfer her father's accounts to an offshore account only Mark had access to. Then, the world would be rid of the Wells family.

"Hey, Collins, hand me that shovel, would you?" One of the other workers looked up from where he stacked planks.

"Sure." Mark took a shovel from where it leaned against the metal building being used as a barn and tossed it. It landed near the man's feet.

"Hey, Dude! You almost hit me." He shook his head and returned to his job.

No thank you. See if he'd help that guy again. He ducked his head and smiled, envisioning himself killing everyone who ticked him off. Every person who got in his way. He glared at the back of the foreman who headed toward Parker. Starting with him.

~

"Mrs. White is looking for you." Colt rested his right foot on the bottom step.

"Oh, no." She snapped shut the book in her hand. "I've forgotten the time." She dashed inside, returning without the book, and locked the door.

"You expecting someone to rob you?" He arched a brow.

"One never knows. I have my father's records in there." She motioned with her head toward the group of working men. "What if one of them is the killer?"

"They've all been cleared."

"Just because they don't have a record doesn't mean they didn't kill my parents and Tanya." She jumped off the porch and headed for the main house.

He fell into step beside her. "You seemed very engrossed in your book."

"My father's journal. Full of mundane daily tasks, some innermost thoughts…" she sighed. "It brings him back to me for a while."

He felt bad about pulling her away, but with Marilyn gone, the ranch cook needed Parker's help. "See you at supper."

Walking next to her had seemed like second nature, not something he wanted to fall back into. Parker worked on the ranch, nothing more. He couldn't let the wounded glint in her eyes when she spoke about her parents get to him. She'd grow bored of the ranch life soon enough and be on her way.

He studied the workers. What if Parker was right? Working on the ranch allowed them access to her. Colt needed to find a way to keep her away from the men. Anyone who got close to her then would rouse suspicion.

His heart faltered as images of the last woman he'd failed filled his mind. Somehow, he'd find a way to keep Parker safe. In order to do so, he'd have to spend time with her. Which meant steeling his heart. Something he could do. He was a special-ops, ex-Marine after all. He knew how to shut off his emotions.

Needing to settle his jumble of thoughts, he stepped into the barn and headed for Crystal, his white mare. "You're the only girl I need, aren't you?" He rubbed her muzzle.

She leaned her head on his shoulder. "How about we go for a ride? I took your brother out last time, but you're my favorite."

She nickered as if she understood him and tossed her head.

"Okay, girl. We'll head out right after supper. I'll bring you an apple." Emotions soothed, he returned to work.

The ringing of the supper bell pulled him away from cleaning horse hooves. He washed up in the water trough, then joined the other ranch hands in the kitchen since the construction workers had gone for the day.

"Want me to saddle Crystal for you?" Willy glanced up from his bowl of stew. "Saw you talking to her."

"I can do it, thanks." He sat at one end of the table.

"Crystal is a horse?" Parker set a bowl in front of him. "If you're going riding, can I come? You know I love to ride. Is there a horse I can use whenever I have time?"

"Just ask any of the hands. They'll fix you up."

"Okay, but what about tonight?"

"You'll be helping Mrs. White during the time I'm riding." He bent over his stew without looking at her, knowing there'd be a pained look on her face. "And no riding alone." That was asking for danger to come knocking.

"I'm sure any one of these fine men would accompany me, am I right?"

Yeps rang out.

He tamped down the seed of jealousy rising in him. At least she wouldn't be alone. Any of the ranch hands were capable of keeping her safe. He'd make sure to let them all know not to leave the grounds. She might throw a fit, but he didn't care. The sheriff had asked him to look after her, and that's what he intended to do. His hand holding the spoon paused on the way to his mouth. Palming her off on someone else was not doing what the sheriff asked. "Fine. I'll wait for you." His shoulders slumped.

The two of them had spent many weekends riding.

It had been one of his favorite pastimes with her. The last thing he wanted to do was ride with her again. He finished eating and sought solace in the barn again. Daisy, the horse the boss's wife had learned to ride on, would be fine for Parker. Yes, she knew how to ride and rode well, but Daisy wouldn't be spurred to gallop, thus preventing Parker from pulling too far ahead of Colt.

If he lost sight of her, the killer would have a prime opportunity to make his move.

Chapter Eight

Parker woke with a smile on her face. For the last few nights, Colt had accompanied her on a horseback ride. He always stayed a little behind her, but he still came along, which gave her hope that someday maybe he would forgive her, and they could start over.

A knock on her bedroom door had her catapulting from the bed. She yanked it open with a grin, fully hoping to see Colt standing there.

Instead, Mrs. White thrust a single red rose and a card at her. "Found these on the front porch of the main house with your name. Looks like you have an admirer. Marilyn is back, so no need to rush to the kitchen."

"Thank you." Parker turned the card over in her hands. While her heart wanted the rose to be from Colt, instinct told her it wasn't. She sat on the edge of her bed and opened the card.

Roses are red, Violets are blue, don't worry, darling, I'm coming for you.

She dropped the card, sending it fluttering to the floor. The rose lay like a blotch on her bed quilt. As if it would burn her fingers, she picked it up by the stem and dropped it into the garbage.

Parker needed to find Colt. He would know what

to do. She quickly got dressed, slid the card into the pocket of her jeans, and dashed toward cottage number one. After several seconds of frantic knocking, she realized Colt wasn't home. She turned and surveyed the surrounding area.

His horse grazed in the paddock. Ranch hands in cowboy hats and boots worked at their morning chores. No sign of Colt. Where was he? She needed him!

Cupping her hands around her eyes, she peered through his front window. If he wasn't outside working, he had to be home. She rapped on the window.

Oh. Her mouth dropped open as he stepped into the kitchen wrapped in nothing but a large blue and white striped towel. She stepped back and spun around to leave.

"It's okay." He opened the door, retreating to his bedroom loft when she entered. "Give me five minutes." He glanced back over his shoulder, then stopped. "What is it?"

She cleared her throat and shook her head. "It can wait. I'll…uh…make coffee." The tiny galley-style kitchen offered little reprieve as her mind whirled with Colt getting dressed over her head. Completely inappropriate thoughts. *Lord, help me.*

"Tell me." Colt stepped into view, buttoning a blue and black plaid shirt. "I can tell from your face something is wrong."

"Mrs. White gave me this. Said it was left on the front porch of the main house. It came with a single red rose."

His features hardened as he read the message. A muscle ticked in his jaw. "We have to give this to the sheriff. Maybe he can pull some prints that aren't yours, mine, or Mrs. White's. Where's the rose?"

"I threw it in the garbage. Do you want it?" She poured coffee into a cup. Her hands shook hard enough to spill some on the counter, and she reached for a paper towel.

"Let me. Sit down before you fall down." Colt lowered her into a chair and took over pouring them coffee and cleaning the spill before sitting across from her. "Have you received anything else like this?"

"No. I'd have told you if I did." Her eyes burned as she lifted her gaze to his. "You're the only one I trust to help me."

"Sheriff Westbrook can help more than I can."

"He doesn't live two doors down." She sniffed and wiped away the tears that had escaped despite her resolve not to cry in front of him. "I'm scared. This man is close. Real close. He could've easily left this note on *my* porch. Been outside *my* front door."

He paled. "I'll contact my boss, then set up a schedule to have the ranch hands patrol the perimeter. The next time this person tries to leave you a message, we'll catch him." He put a hand over hers. "I promise."

She relished the warmth of his hand over hers. "That's a promise you might not be able to keep."

"I always keep my promises, remember?" The corner of his mouth twitched.

She took a deep, shuddering breath. "I'm counting on it." Her coffee untouched, she pushed to her feet. "I'll go call the sheriff."

"Let me know when he arrives if you don't want to speak to him alone." He returned the card to her.

"I'm not afraid of the man." She chuckled. "Westbrook's the stern type, but I guess that comes with the job. He seems fair."

"He is."

"Thank you." Parker headed home to where she'd left her cell phone and dialed the sheriff's department. The receptionist promised he'd be at the ranch within the hour. Rather than wait and dwell on her "gift," she went to the kitchen to help with breakfast.

The sheriff arrived during the meal.

Parker shoved her half-eaten plate of scrambled eggs aside and joined him outside. Colt followed a second later.

After explaining about the gift, she handed the sheriff the note. "The rose is in the garbage, but I can get it if you want."

"I'll take a photo of it. That'll be fine. How many have touched this?" He dropped the card into a small evidence bag.

"Four counting you and whoever left it. Me, Colt, Mrs. White...oh, five." She sagged against the railing. "He was right here." She stared at the boards under her feet. Where would he go next? Her house? Catch her alone in the barn or on a walk? Stop her on her way into town?

The construction workers started arriving, putting a halt to the conversation. Colt left to go over the day's priorities while Parker led the sheriff to the rose.

He took a photo. "I'll be in touch."

"You don't expect to find out anything, do you?" She crossed her arms and tilted her head.

"Unless this man's prints are on the card and in the system, no. I'm sorry. Don't go anywhere alone, Miss Wells."

~

Mark suppressed the desire to laugh out loud as he strolled past the big front porch with the other men. Parker had called the sheriff. He couldn't wait to send her another gift, and another, until she longed to come face-to-face with him and end the terror. He eyed her house as he passed. Next time, he'd leave the gift there. There was no need to wait until nightfall. He could find time during the day, drop it in a place where she'd see it, but nobody else could. Oh, the fun!

Having this much fun dispelled some of the urgency of killing her. That would come. For now, he'd enjoy the fear that radiated off her. He hadn't been able to experience that thrill with her parents.

He got in line with a few of the men to lift one wall of studs into place for the barn. Progress moved a lot faster than he wanted it to. Once the barn was finished, he'd have no reason to be on the ranch unless they were hiring ranch hands, which he doubted.

Maybe he needed to sabotage the progress on the barn—start things over at some point. Anything to keep him coming to the ranch until he accomplished his mission.

For right now, he'd wait until Parker saw the gift that would be arriving that afternoon.

~

Colt couldn't concentrate on the emails on the laptop. His mind kept going back to the threatening note Parker received. He was foreman of the ranch—the man in charge until Dylan came home, but he hadn't been able to prevent a killer from stepping foot on the front porch.

A glance at his watch sent him to the bunkhouse. He'd asked the others to gather there for a meeting before lunch.

They listened stoically as he told them about the rose and the note.

"This is a bit of déjà vu," Clay Jenkins said. "One of us might end up like Bill Washington not too long ago."

"You saying you don't want to help?" Colt frowned.

"No, just making sure we all know the risk."

Colt looked at each of them in turn, Maverick Browning, Clay Jenkins, Deacon Simpson, Ryder Barton, Lincoln Stone, Willy Billings, and River Swanson. All ex-military men who had seen hell and come out on the other side. "It's a lot to ask," he said.

"Not really." Maverick shrugged. "Parker is one of us now. We watch out for our own. I'll work out a schedule."

"Thanks. Make sure to put me in the rotation. Shouldn't have to do more than an hour each. Now, let's get lunch." The bell rang, putting an end to the short meeting. "Don't go smothering Parker. You'll only frighten her more."

The men trooped out of the bunkhouse toward the tent used for the midday meal. The construction workers had lined up to fill their plates with burgers, hot dogs, and potato salad. Parker stood off to one side, nibbling on some potato chips.

The ranch hands sent glances her way, but none approached her. Good. Colt knew he could count on them. He scanned the line of construction workers. Was one of them the one who'd left the rose? Their boss still didn't have all the background checks in. What if Colt had a killer right under his nose? One bent on ridding the world of Parker Wells?

Several of them met his eyes and gave him a nod before finding a place at the long table. None of them seemed to pay Parker much attention. No one looked like a killer, but then, neither had the infamous Ted Bundy.

He filled a plate of his own and sat in the empty chair nearest Parker. Whether he wanted to be close to her or not had been decided for him. The danger to her had escalated. He didn't think for a moment that the killer would stick to leaving gifts. No, things would start to pick up pace, and that thought scared his blood cold.

Parker's shoulders heaved, then she grabbed a hot dog and carried it to her house. She stopped at the bottom step, then whipped around to face him.

The wide-eyed look on her face had him rushing to her side. Her gaze flicked to the porch. He peered into the box there.

A tiny black and white kitten peered up at him. At the bottom of the box lay a single red rose.

Colt whirled. How had someone with a cat walked right past them without being seen? "Come with me." He gripped her arm.

"But the kitten." She pulled free. "I can't leave it out here alone."

Colt grabbed the box. "Come on." He strode to the big house and into the kitchen. "Did someone make a delivery?"

Marilyn nodded. "A few minutes ago. Left it on the front porch of the main house. Looks like Parker has an admirer." She wiggled her eyebrows. "I thought it would be a nice surprise for her to find it outside her own door."

He thrust the box at her. "Get rid of it. From now on, all deliveries to Parker go through me."

"No way." Parker took the kitten from the box. "I'm keeping this sweet thing. It isn't this poor kitten's fault a killer dropped it off."

"A killer?" Marilyn reached for the neckline of her apron.

"I think there's some news you need to tell us." Mrs. White glared. "Is it time to start carrying my gun in my apron pocket again?"

"Yes, ma'am, it is." He stared at the cat. "Are you sure you want to keep it? Won't it be a reminder that someone wishes you harm?"

"It's just a kitten, Colt." She nuzzled the little thing. "I'm going to call him Tuxedo. I need to go into town for some supplies."

"Order a delivery which I will inspect once it gets here." He eyed each of the women. "Do we understand?"

"Sure do." Mrs. White grinned. "I'm always up for a little spice in my day."

"This isn't a game." How could they take this so lightly? "This is the second so-called gift today."

"And there will be more before it's all said and down, my dear. No sense in hiding. We'll keep an eye on our Parker, never fear. This isn't the first storm to arrive on the ranch. We'll weather it same as the last one."

Colt hoped her words rang true.

Chapter Nine

A thud jerked Parker away. Her gaze dashed from one corner of her loft to another. Tuxedo meowed and burrowed under the blankets.

When the sound came again, Parker sat upright. Someone was on her front porch. Leaving another gift or something more deadly?

She eyed her phone on the nightstand, tempted to call Colt. What if the noise was simply the wind? Was it just her imagination after receiving the ominous warning the day before? She needed to make sure before she overreacted.

Parker landed softly on bare feet as she slid from the bed. "You stay here." She patted the kitten under the covers wishing they would shield her as well from the evil at bay.

A shadow crossed, outlined through her window shades by her porch light. There was someone there! Who was patrolling the ranch? Why hadn't they seen this person?

She tiptoed to the kitchen and slid a butcher knife from a drawer. It's what the heroine did in all the movies. Why couldn't it work for her?

Hand trembling, she approached the door only to

be meant with silence. She held her breath and waited. A few seconds later, there was another thud, then the scrape of something by the small kitchen window. None of the windows in the tiny house were big enough for an adult to squeeze through except for the one in the loft. The only other entrance was the front door. What did this person intend to do?

When the sounds came from the back of her house, she dashed out the front door, leaped off the porch, and raced for Colt's house. After a frantic pounding on the door, she plastered her back to his wall, knife held in front of her, and strained to see through the dark.

Her breath caught in her throat as footsteps crunched the gravel around the house. He was coming for her! She closed her eyes, then snapped them open. Not waiting to be cornered, she made a mad dash for the closest building. The tin barn.

The door squeaked open when she tugged on it. She inched it closed and waited for her eyes to adjust to the dimness. A nightlight, activated by motion, glowed from one high corner. Enough to let someone who entered after her see just fine.

If she didn't move, the light would stay off until someone else entered. She'd have some warning in order to react.

Still clutching the knife, she found an empty horse stall and slid to a crouch in the far corner. The dust and straw tickled her nose. Do not sneeze, please do not sneeze. She sneezed, then froze. No sound of the barn door opening. The small side door, the one closest to her, always opened with a click, but she'd overheard the men say they kept that one locked at night. She kept her focus on the main door.

There were only so many places to look for her. The main house would be locked, and she doubted the intruder would risk trying to enter there. Once he ruled out the tiny houses and the bunkhouse, he'd come here.

Her hand grew moist around the handle of the knife. Could she even use it if someone came after her with the intent to kill? She hoped she wasn't one of those meek women who fainted rather than fought.

Parker put a hand to her chest as if she could keep her heart from beating free. Her breath came in gasps. She very well might faint after all. *Why is this happening, Daddy? Why did someone kill you? Why do they want me dead?* Tears burned her eyes.

No. She Would…Not…Cry. *A Wells never gives up. They never show weakness.* She pulled her knees to her chest, realizing she'd wore satin shorts and a camisole to bed. Great. She'd die in her girly pajamas with tears streaking down her face. Colt was right. She was pampered and spoiled. Now was not the time to evaluate her shortcomings. She could do that in the morning…if she lived that long.

Hiding under the covers sounded better by each passing second. At least then, she'd die in her bed instead of in the barn like an animal. She wrapped her arms around her knees and rested her forehead on them. Breathe in, breathe out.

How long had it been? Maybe whoever was on patrol scared the person away. How long should she stay before venturing out?

She sneezed again, a slight wheeze sounding in her chest. Wonderful. She hadn't had asthma problems in years. Now, when it was most inconvenient, the hay triggered it. Parker glared at the straw she sat in, then slowly got to her feet. She needed to get out while she could still breathe.

The barn door slid open.

With as much of a primal scream as she could muster with her lungs sounding like a squeaky screen door, she raised the knife and pounced from the stall.

~

"Whoa!" Colt jumped back and gripped Parker's wrist. "Give me that." He took the knife from her hand. "Mind telling me what's going on?"

"Outside."

At the sound of her wheeze, he scooped her into his arms and outside. "Do you have an inhaler?"

She nodded. "Nightstand."

He raced for her house and deposited her on the sofa before thundering up her stairs. He found an inhaler in the nightstand. The label had been worn off. How old was the thing? He couldn't remember ever seeing her with one before. Colt rushed back to her side and handed it to her.

She took one puff, held her breath, released it, and took another. "Thanks."

"I didn't know you had asthma." Concern filled him.

"It hasn't bothered me in a long time." She let out a long slow breath.

"Mind telling me why now, and why you were in the barn with a butcher knife?" Which he'd dropped on the floor of the barn before gathering her in his arms.

"Someone was outside my house. I went looking for you, and when I couldn't find you, I hid in the barn." She rested her head back against the sofa.

His gaze slid down her body. "Get dressed, Parker,

while I look around outside." Before he lost self-control and kissed her until they were both out of their heads in love.

While she changed, he searched the kitchen drawers for a flashlight. Finding a small one, he moved outside and circled the building.

No footprints appeared in the dirt, but it hadn't rained in a while. He found an area where gravel had been moved. Marks that looked like Parker's bare feet digging in, then gravel flinging as she ran. He couldn't see whether anyone had actually been outside her house, but something had definitely frightened her enough to run and hide while clutching a butcher knife.

He surveyed the area around the house, expanding his gaze toward the tree line where he'd been patrolling while Parker ran scared out of her mind.

"See anything?" She whispered behind him, almost making him jump.

He turned and frowned. "Is that a paring knife?"

"You dropped my other one."

"Give me that." He held out his hand.

"Fine, but I'm going with you." She dropped the knife into his palm.

"What makes you think I'm going anywhere?"

"Aren't you?"

"Yes." He sighed. She knew he wouldn't be able to sleep until whoever was sneaking around her house was gone. "Stay behind me. If something happens, run as fast as you can for the house. Mrs. White and the other ranch hands will come running if you ring the cowbell. How's your breathing?"

"I'm fine. Just a reaction to the dust and the hay." She coughed on cue.

"Right." He took her hand in his, and they set off at a run, sticking to the perimeter of the cleared land around the house and outbuildings. They stayed in the shadows as much as possible. "I should've asked before, but do you have your phone on you?"

"Yes, you?"

"Yep." He expected all the cowboys to carry theirs while on patrol. "Dial the sheriff's office. Report an intruder."

"What if the intruder is gone?"

"It will still be on the record that he was here." He led her just inside the tree line. "Help me look for footprints, broken branches—anything to signify someone ran through here. We'll keep going until we reach the open field again." He sent a text to Willy to wake up the other men and have them search all the buildings. If the intruder was still on the ranch, he'd be found.

Colt waved the flashlight back and forth across the ground in front of them. A mashed area of grass, then another, leading deeper into the trees or coming out, he couldn't be sure. He stopped and looked across the expanse of pasture.

Whoever had stood there had a clear view of Parker's house. He glanced into the treetops searching for the cameras Dylan had installed when his wife Dani had been in danger. No red light blinked from them.

Which could only mean one thing. Someone had cut the power to the house's Wi-Fi. There'd be no capture of the person on camera.

Colt's phone buzzed. He pulled it from his pocket and glanced at the screen. Willy replied that the men were up and out.

"Sheriff is on his way," Parker whispered. "Or one of his deputies. I'm not sure, really. Does it matter? I wouldn't think it would—"

Colt put a finger over her lips. "You're rambling, darlin'. It's going to be okay. The man is gone."

"Are you sure?" Her lips moved against his finger as her eyes filled with tears.

"Ninety-percent sure." He wrapped his free arm around her. "I'm here, Parker. No one is going to hurt you." He closed his eyes and rested his chin on top of her head. At least, he'd do his darned best not to let anything happen to her.

She wrapped her arms around his waist and leaned her cheek against his shoulder as she'd done so many times in the past. Whenever something had upset her, he'd hold her just like this, minus the knife and flashlight.

He raised his eyes heavenward. *What are you doing to me?* The cold wall around his heart started to melt. With that, the pain of Parker's rejection came to life. It would take time for him to move past the fact she'd chosen money over him.

From the direction of the house came the flashing of red and blue lights. "Time to go." He set her at arm's length and stared into her face. "You okay?"

"I am now," she said, her words husky. "I'm always okay when I'm with you."

"You're killing me, Parker." He dropped the flashlight and knife and cupped her face. "I have so many questions that need answering, but now is not the time." His gaze fell to her lips. Before he could succumb to his urges, he backed away and retrieved the items he'd dropped. "I'll fetch the butcher knife from the barn after the sheriff leaves."

"Okay." Confusion laced her reply. "We'll talk when you're ready."

With a nod, he headed toward the flashing lights.

Chapter Ten

After a long, restless night dreaming of faceless men chasing her through the dark, Parker sat up and reached for her father's journal. So far, she'd found nothing to give her a clue as to who might have wanted him dead.

She read a few more pages, then flipped through them, scanning for clues. The back page stuck to the binding. She inserted her fingernail behind the page and slowly peeled it from the back cover.

Words in her father's handwriting were scrawled across the back of the page. He'd glued the page down purposefully.

Parker adjusted her bedside lamp for a better look and held the book under the light. "Answers are found where the snow flies."

What snow? It was the middle of summer in Arkansas.

Hope built to a crescendo. Her first clue. She jumped from the bed and raced for the shower. The only snow she knew about was her snow-globe collection boxed up and waiting for her to retrieve from her parents' attic. Since today was her only day off in a while, she'd head to Little Rock and do some digging.

She practically floated into the kitchen, dressed in a loose, flowing summer dress and her pink cowboy boots. "I'm headed to Little Rock after breakfast. Anyone need anything?"

"I have some time. I'll go with you." The look on Colt's face left no room for argument.

"Okay." She shrugged, secretly pleased. Despite her sleepless night, his veiled promise the night before had left her with a warm fuzzy feeling. He did still care for her but was too afraid to show his feelings.

"Did you forget Sheriff Westbrook said you weren't to go anywhere alone?"

There it was. She sighed. The real reason he'd volunteered to go with her. Last night had been nothing more than fear in the moment. "I haven't forgotten. Why do you think I brought it up?" *Liar.* She hadn't spared the sheriff's order a second thought in her excitement to finally have a clue. Parker grabbed a bowl of oatmeal and sat at the table across from him. "Can you leave right after we eat?"

"Yep." He set his spoon in his bowl and stood. "Meet me at the truck when you're ready." His intense gaze settled on her for a moment before he placed his dishes in the sink and headed outside.

"That man sure is surly around you," Mrs. White said. "Still has feelings for you is my opinion."

"Of that I have no doubt. They just aren't the type of feelings you think they are." Parker ate quickly, ignoring the questioning gazes of the other cowboys, then handed over her dirty dishes and raced to her house to collect her purse and the journal. Purse slung over her shoulder, she joined Colt at his truck, climbing in before he could come around to open the door for her. "Thank you for driving."

He nodded. "What's in the rock that you can't get in town here?"

"My snow globes."

"As in Christmas ones? I've seen your snow globes. You have at least twenty."

"I found a clue in my father's journal that said, 'Answers are found where the snow flies.' That's the only snow I can think of at this time of the year." She clicked her seatbelt into place. "Hence the trip to the attic."

He narrowed his eyes. "Why are you being so cryptic?"

"I was saving the info for the long drive." She flashed him a grin. "Now, we have nothing to talk about."

Shaking his head, he turned the key in the ignition, then flipped on the radio. Country music played from the speakers. "Fine with me."

She pouted and crossed her arms. "Guess I'll catch up on some sleep." She shot him a glare, then leaned her seat back as far as it would go. When she closed her eyes, the same nightmare from the night before flashed through her mind. *I need to think about something good. Snow globes are good.* Parker remembered each Christmas when she found a new one under the tree. Her parents had purchased them from all across the world. Colt was right. She had over twenty, one for each year of her life. Twenty-six to be exact. Which one would hold the clue her father had left?

Why leave her a clue? Had he known his life was in danger? Her eyes snapped open. He must have known. Why else leave the clue in the journal? He had to know that Parker would eventually go through the boxes from his business, but he probably didn't think it would take her six months of procrastinating. If Tanya hadn't been killed, Parker still would have put off the task.

Going through their drawers, cleaning out their closets, disposing of their things…only brought their deaths to the forefront of her mind. In true pampered-princess fashion, she'd rather forget it had happened at all. Now, with someone after her, she had no choice but to face the fact her parents were gone—most likely murdered, Tanya was definitely murdered, which left it up to Parker to find their killer.

The least qualified person in Arkansas.

"What's with all the sighing?"

She peered at Colt. "Just facing reality." She returned her seat to its upright position. "It's up to me to catch my parents' killer."

"No, it's up to the authorities." He glanced at her as if she'd sprouted horns. "Whatever we might find today goes directly to them. If not, you could be arrested for impeding a murder investigation."

"They still don't believe my parents were murdered."

"No, but they believe your friend was. Eventually, the pieces will all fit together. Especially with the reports Sheriff Westbrook sends to LRPD."

"Fine." Parker agreed in principle, but that didn't mean she'd stop snooping on her end. The authorities moved way too slowly. She didn't want to die because they didn't find the culprit in time. Her gut told her she'd need a weapon in the near future. She would also retrieve the Ruger her father taught her to shoot with.

~

Colt didn't believe Parker for a second. She'd given in too easily. The woman had something on her mind he definitely wouldn't like.

By the time he pulled the truck up the winding drive of her family home, his mind had spun all sorts of possibilities, ranging from her running away to facing the killer alone. Both possibilities sent a trickle of perspiration down his spine.

Together, they approached the front door. Parker pulled a key from her purse. A light blinked from the control panel to the alarm as they entered, and she punched in the code to turn it off.

The musty smell of a house closed up for months assailed his nostrils. What did Parker intend to do with this massive house? It had to be worth a fortune.

Parker squared her shoulders and headed up the wide staircase to the second floor. She stopped in the doorway to her parents' room. Silent sobs shook her, before she turned and opened a door halfway down a hallway. Wooden stairs rose to the attic.

It took all his self-control not to pull her into his arms as he had the night before and kiss away her sorrow. Last night should not have happened. He wouldn't make the same mistake twice. The feel of her in his arms had kept him awake for hours.

At the top of the stairs, Parker flipped a switch which lit up the attic. "The box is over here." She led him to the opposite corner and opened a large cardboard box full of smaller white boxes. "I have no idea which one he meant. This might take a while."

"—If your assumption is right." He knelt on the dusty floor while she pulled up a chair covered with a sheet. "I'll hand you a couple. With both of us looking, it shouldn't take too long."

Last Christmas, he'd given her the snow globe he held in his hand. One that he'd spent a long time online picking out. A man and a woman strolling hand in hand through a snowy landscape. He'd foolishly thought the couple resembled him and Parker. Colt turned it over in his hand and removed the battery plate. Nothing.

Soon, they had a pile of snow-globe boxes around them.

"If not these, then what could he mean?" Parker stood and stretched, her eyes scanning each corner of the attic.

"Something else that has to do with snow. Skiing?" Colt grunted as he stood. He was too old to sit on the floor for long periods of time.

"My family aren't skiers." She paced, her steps leaving prints in the dust. "But—" She rushed to another box and dropped to her knees. "We did spend a week in upstate New York once. It snowed quite a bit." She opened a box and pulled out a photo album.

"It could be we're looking in the wrong place."

She frowned. "Don't be a Debbie Downer. The clue is in this attic somewhere. I feel it." She slipped through pages, looking behind every photo. When she reached the last place, she sat back, letting the album slide to the floor. "Hold on. My father went on a business trip once and complained about the weather. He'd been snowed in at his hotel for days. A newspaper article had been written about the conference he attended. Mom kept all that sort of memorabilia. The question is where? There are a lot of boxes up here."

"We'd better keep looking. Mind if I open them

without you?"

She waved a hand. "Sure. I've nothing to hide at this point, and we'll go faster if we focus on different boxes."

He headed for the opposite side of the attic to where boxes that had once held copy paper were stacked. These looked like they might have come from an office. The first box proved him right. "These look like they might have belonged to your father."

"More business boxes?" Her eyes widened. "I still haven't finished with the ones I had delivered from his office."

"These are older." He scooted a box her way. "Happy digging."

"Colt—" Several boxes later, she held up a newspaper. "Here is the article I was talking about. There's a photo of Dad and two of his employees, but the heavy snowfall makes it hard to distinguish their features."

"What does the article say?"

She read for a few minutes, then glanced up with wide eyes. "It wasn't a business trip. My father was being investigated for embezzlement. He wouldn't, Colt. I know he wouldn't."

"Don't jump to conclusions." He took the paper from her hands and read it for himself. "He went there for questioning. We need to find out what the courts determined." *If* it went to court. "My gut tells me this is the key. If your father didn't embezzle anything, then somebody else did, and that someone—"

"Would kill to keep their identity unknown." She paled. "Tanya was killed as a warning to me. The killer must suspect I'd go digging and might discover his identity."

"Which we haven't, but he won't know that." Colt folded the paper and stuffed it into his back pocket. "Maybe LRPD will have more information on this. There has to be records other than this article if there was an investigation into the alleged charges."

She nodded, then gasped. "Colt..." She pointed at the stairs.

He turned.

Smoke curled over the edge of the floor and crawled toward them.

Chapter Eleven

"My house!" Parker ran for the stairs.

"Stop." Colt grabbed her arm and pulled her to a halt. "Let me take a look first."

"My house can't burn; it just can't. It's all I have left of my parents." Her words broke on a sob, then a cough.

Colt peered over the top of the attic stairs. "I don't see flames, but stay behind me anyway."

Tears streamed from her eyes, both from fear and the smoke. The house had insurance, but all her childhood memories were in the attic or her bedroom closet downstairs. They had to keep the house from burning.

"I don't see any flames." Once Colt reached the bottom of the stairs, he held out a hand to help Parker.

"Then, where's the smoke coming from?" She coughed again.

He shrugged, then moved around the corner into the hall. "Parker."

She followed. At his feet lay an almost depleted smoke bomb. "Why would someone—"

He yanked her into the nearest room, a bathroom. "Someone lured us from that attic." He closed the door, then moved to the window.

"There's no way down. Believe me, I would've used it during high school." Parker sat on the closed toilet lid.

"I don't see anyone, but I have a very bad feeling about this. I'm calling the police. We can stay in—"

The window shattered. He yelped and ducked, putting a hand to his head. His fingers came away sticky with blood.

"You're shot!"

"No, it's just from the glass fragments. Stay down." He crawled toward her.

"Let me see." She reached for him, fear threatening to choke her.

"I'm fine. You can doctor me later." He pushed her hand down.

"But, we're in a room with a medicine cabinet." She frowned. "I can…"

"Sweetheart, now is not the time." He cupped her cheek. "Let me figure out how to get us out of here alive." He dialed 911 on his phone and placed a call for help.

"We can't stay here. We're sitting ducks." Parker stood. "This time, let me be the hero. My father thought it cool to put secret passages in the house to help occupy me. I can get us outside easily enough. Then it'll be up to you to get us to your truck." She held out her hand. "Do you trust me?"

The expression on his face said otherwise, but he nodded and took her hand. He pulled his gun from the back waistband of his pants. "Lead on."

Staying low, she led him from the bathroom.

Footsteps sounded downstairs. The shooter had

reentered the house.

Parker headed for a closet in one of the guestrooms and pushed against the back wall. A secret door swung open. She grabbed a flashlight from a shelf her father had built and turned it on. The batteries were low, but the flashlight still offered enough light to make their way.

The passageway narrowed into stairs that led to the first floor. Parker pressed her ear against the door at the end, then slowly eased the door open. Not seeing anyone, she dashed for her mother's sitting room and into another secret passage. This one led to the basement.

"This is the coolest house," Colt whispered.

"I always thought so." The flashlight flickered out. No matter. She knew the secret way through the house with her eyes closed.

This time they stepped into the basement. Sheets covered the pool table and foosball table. After high school, few people had reason to visit the basement, but during Parker's teen years, she'd held a lot of parties down there.

She stepped to the side while Colt moved to the window just above her head. He looked out, turning his head this way and that.

Feet encased in work boots shuffled overhead, freezing Parker and Colt in place. When the feet moved on, Parker slowly released the breath she'd held.

Sirens wailed, followed by the pounding of footsteps.

"Looks like he's leaving," she said, putting a hand to her racing heart.

"Let's give it a few more minutes before we leave

the safety of the basement."

"Okay." Her breath wheezed. Oh, no. Her purse was in Colt's truck. She counted and took deep slow breaths, willing her breathing back to normal. After years of no asthma problems, why would her childhood ailment kick back in now? Answer: More than regular physical activity. Dust and hay in ready supply at the ranch. Plenty of dust in the attic. Not to mention danger. Lots of danger. She sat in a sheet-covered chair and did her best to expand her lungs.

Colt pulled her inhaler from his pocket. "I brought it just in case. Forgive me for snatching it out of your purse, but I saw it sitting on top, and the purse was open."

She inhaled the medicine and leaned her head back. "Thank you...for...invading my...privacy."

"Anytime." He shot her a wink that almost stopped her heart, then turned back to the window. "Cops are here. I think it's safe to go out. We're going to stop at the drugstore on our way out of town. You need a new inhaler."

"Yes, Boss." She pushed to her feet, her breathing coming easier now. "We'll buy stuff to take care of those cuts on your face, too. Might as well buy fresh supplies. The ones here are who knows how old." She was rambling but couldn't help it. As they went upstairs, adrenaline rushed through her veins like a tornado. Her hands shook, and her head pounded.

Thank God, Colt was with her.

~

Mark sat next to his mother who stared out the window as if he weren't sitting next to her. Her Alzheimer's had progressed rapidly until she spent more time inside her head than out. One more reason he hated the Wells family.

He'd needed that money to afford the best medical attention money could buy. Without it, she'd had to rely on state funding. Nowhere near good enough.

"I'm sorry, Mama. I did my best." He patted her hand.

She didn't respond; she barely blinked. Despite weekly Sunday visits, his only day not working on the ranch lately, he rarely spent time with her. She didn't know him after all, but he visited enough for the staff to remark on how he was such a devoted son.

He relished the accolades.

"Those responsible will pay, Mama. Only one more, and that horrible family will no longer exist. It might not bring you back to me, but it'll provide some consolation nevertheless." He leaned over and planted a kiss on her cool cheek. "In case you slip away before next Sunday, goodbye, Mama."

~

The detective listened as Colt talked, then showed him the newspaper article. "This is still an active investigation taking a second spot to the murder of Miss Wells' friend. As of today, we have no proof whether Mr. Wells embezzled from the firm or whether someone else did. I suggest the two of you let us handle things before you get yourselves killed."

"I have every right to be in my parents' home, Detective." Parker crossed her arms. "I do have to go through their things at some point."

"Yes, ma'am, but not with the intent of finding their alleged killer." He returned his gaze to Colt. "I expect you to know better, being ex-military PD."

"Special forces."

"My mistake. The two of you go home. Seek medical attention for those cuts, Mr. Dawson. Let us do our jobs."

Dismissed, Colt turned to Parker. "There's nothing more for us to do here. Not today."

"Agreed. I have no desire to go back inside so soon after being shot at. We'll come back next week." She narrowed her eyes. "Next time, let's do a better job of not being followed."

He hadn't expected to be followed at all. Parker must be getting close to finding out the truth about her parents. Which meant their killer was getting worried and would up his game at shutting her up for good. The thought chilled Colt's blood. Parker might not have chosen him in the grand scheme of things, but he couldn't imagine a world without her.

His stinging face reminded him they still had a stop to make before heading back to the ranch. "Let's take care of business, grab some fast food, and get home." He placed his hand on the small of her back and led her to his truck, more than ready to leave her childhood home behind. Today had left one more bad taste in his mouth. The last time he'd stepped foot there was the time Parker had said goodbye.

At the drugstore, he purchased the supplies needed to clean his cuts while Parker refilled a prescription for her inhaler. Since the prescription had expired, they had some time to wait.

"Come with me." He led her to the men's room. After taking a peek inside, he held the door open.

"I can't go in there." She took a step back.

"You can't stay out here, and I need the sink. No one is inside. It's fine." He jerked his head for her to enter.

"This is embarrassing." She glanced around. "I hope no one sees me."

He shook his head and followed her inside, locking the door behind them. "They'll think we're up to no good." He grinned and set the supplies on the sink.

"Need help?" She leaned against the wall.

"Nope." He washed his face with soap from the wall dispenser, dried off with paper towels, then applied ointment. None of the cuts were deep and wouldn't leave scars. They were lucky. Things could've been a lot worse.

Finished, he returned the leftover supplies to the pharmacy bag, then unlocked the bathroom door. He peered out before declaring it safe.

"My inhaler is ready." Parker stepped past him, then stopped.

Colt glanced up as surprised to see Mark Collins as he was to see them. He glanced down, noting the work boots. Footwear exactly like the ones that had passed the attic window. He narrowed his eyes. "What brings you to Little Rock, Mark?"

"I come every Sunday to visit my mother. She's in a nursing home." He glowered. "Not that my free time is any of your business."

"Which nursing home?"

"Perpetual Hope. Why the third degree?"

"If I were to call there, can they verify you were there?"

His eyes narrowed. "Look, man. I don't appreciate you grilling me. I came in here to pick up some deodorant and use the bathroom, and instead I get interrogated." He raised his brows. "I could ask why the two of you were in here together. A bit unseemly, if you ask me. Rumors could start about the two of you."

"Unseemly?" Parker shook her head. "We aren't living in Victorian England. Come on, Colt. Let's get my inhaler and head home. I've had enough excitement for one day." She marched to the pharmacy window.

Colt followed, glancing over his shoulder as Mark entered the bathroom. The man stopped and met Colt's gaze with a cold, hard one of his own before closing the door.

While Parker paid for her prescription, Colt looked up the number of the nursing home and dialed it. He wasn't normally a suspicious person, but with all that had been going on, he wasn't taking any chances.

"I'm looking for my buddy, Mark Collins. He's been looking for work, and I have a lead for him. Is he there?"

The receptionist apologized. "He left here about fifteen minutes ago. Comes to visit his mother every Sunday."

"Yes, I know. That's why I thought to try and get a hold of him there. Thank you." Colt hung up. Mark had told the truth. Which meant, he wasn't the man who had shot at them.

He watched the bathroom door until Mark came back out. Something about the man's build bothered him. Not that he was unique, but Colt trusted his instincts, and right now they told him there was more to Mark Collins than he knew.

"I'm ready." She followed his gaze. "Everything okay?"

"Yeah, he checks out." With one last glance at Mark, Colt led Parker from the store back to the truck.

Parker clicked her seatbelt into place. "Did you notice how he smelled like smoke?"

Chapter Twelve

Colt kept an eye on Mark the next day, not caring whether the man knew he watched him or not. He didn't trust him. Not after yesterday.

Sure the man's story about visiting his mother checked out, but there was still something about him that set Colt on edge. The man stepped to the side and lit a cigarette. At least he had the sense not to smoke around the wood and hay, and the cigarette explained why he'd smelled like smoke the day before.

It frustrated him how he and Parker would find one clue that led to finding out the truth, then something explained the idea and made things muddy again. As he pushed a wheelbarrow full of manure to the compost heap, his mind returned to the newspaper article about Parker's father.

Her father had spoken about his company to Colt on many occasions when he'd gone over there for supper. Not once had the man acted nervous at any of Colt's questions. The article had been written after his breakup with Parker.

Could Colt have misjudged him? He'd gotten along with Mr. Wells fine, as much as the man wanting to marry a rich man's daughter could. Then, Parker had told him her parents would disown her if she married him. It had seemed to come out of left field.

He tipped the manure into a pile. It hadn't made sense then, and it didn't make sense now.

A blind man could see the love that still shone from Parker's eyes when she looked at him. It didn't take away the gut-wrenching pain of her betrayal, but it soothed the outer edges of his wound. Would it be so bad to try again with her now that her parents were gone? Maybe not. Something he might consider once the phantom stalking Parker was out of the picture.

As if his thoughts had lured her from the main house, Parker stepped onto the back deck. The ranch dog, Monster, sat at her feet and stared at the bagel in her hand. Parker smiled and broke off a piece for the dog.

Colt turned to her house to see the black and white kitten sitting in the window. Why give her a pet after a warning note? What kind of game was this killer playing?

A floral delivery truck pulled up to the front of the main house. Colt removed his gloves, draping them over the side of the wheelbarrow, then went to intercept it.

A young man stepped out with two vases of flowers.

"I'll take those." Colt went to hand the man a twenty-dollar-bill, then realized he had no free hands. "Sorry." He took one of the vases and tried again.

"Thanks, man." He pocketed the money and gave Colt the other vase.

Colt set both on the front porch where Parker waited. "I'm not going to let you throw away a note without me seeing it." She lifted her chin.

"This bouquet is for Marilyn. From Buster is my guess." He switched from the lavender roses to the dozen red roses and pulled out a card. "Roses are red, violets are blue, I once wanted to marry you." His heart dropped to his knees as he continued reading. "But since it was not to be, I'll admire you from afar…until the moon turns blue, then I'm coming for you."

"What does that mean?" Parker's eyes widened.

"Which? The part about wanting to marry you, or the part about the moon turning blue?" He slipped the card into his pocket to give to the sheriff.

"The moon."

"I'm guessing he means a full moon. Which means, he might act within a month." They'd just had a full moon. If his guess was correct, they had a month before the man acted on his threat. "Who besides me wanted to marry you?"

"No one. There's been no one but you for years." She lowered into an Adirondack chair. "I seriously have no idea." She chewed on her thumb nail. A shadow crossed her eyes. "This note scares me more than the others, despite the poor attempt at poetry. Especially after yesterday." She folded her hands in her lap. "Why try to kill us yesterday if he plans on doing so in the future? Is he playing with us, or has he changed his plans?"

Colt shrugged. "Either or." She wasn't the only one frightened. Not even the skirmishes he'd engaged in while in the Middle East put fear in him like the idea of losing Parker did.

"What do we do?"

"Well…" He took a deep breath, then released it

long and slow. "He's given us a deadline, such as it is. I'm not sure whether that means you're safe until then, or if that's the absolute latest he comes for you."

"I'm going to hire a private investigator to dig into what really happened at that supposed convention. Perhaps a PI can dig up something that points to someone besides my father." She stood.

"That's a good idea. We need all the help we can get. Since I have to call the sheriff anyway, want me to ask for a recommendation?"

"Yes and toss those roses on top of the manure pile." She picked up the ones for Marilyn. "If whoever sent them is watching, let him see what I think about his gift." She carried the lavender roses into the house, leaving Colt with his mouth hanging open.

Parker no longer resembled a spoiled little rich girl. She was quickly growing a backbone. He grinned and pulled his cell phone from his pocket.

~

Mark ducked his head to hide his grin when Colt tossed the roses onto the compost pile. Jealous, cowboy?

It should be against the law to have this much fun. It might not be the smartest thing to put killing Parker off for a month, but she wasn't going anywhere. Neither was he. Might as well enjoy the journey.

He leaned a ladder against the unpainted wall of the new barn under construction and climbed to the roof on the pretense of nailing shingles. In all honesty, the high vantage point let him keep a closer eye on Parker.

Had she found anything in her attic yesterday? Mark had broken into her father's office and found nothing incriminating, which was odd. When Wells had confronted him, telling him to stay away from his daughter and her fiancé, he'd admitted to having evidence against Mark that he wouldn't hesitate to use if he didn't listen. If that evidence had been in the attic, Mark wouldn't still be working on the ranch. He'd be behind bars.

His eyes narrowed as a car from the sheriff's office pulled up to the house. Here to retrieve his latest note. He shook his head. Fools, all of them, not able to see the threat right under their noses. Parker wouldn't be the only person he took down when the time came.

Maybe he'd make sure this ranch never got back on its feet. It would give him one big hoorah before he got what he wanted and retired in Mexico. He shrugged. Dreaming was nice, but at this point, he wanted Parker's money, and he wanted her dead.

~

Later that evening, Parker joined Colt in the barn. "Are we still going for a ride?"

He tightened the cinch on her horse. "Don't we always?"

"I wasn't sure after receiving the note and roses today."

"As long as we stay within sight of the ranch, we should be good. The other ranch hands will be keeping an eye on us." He patted the horse's neck. "These sweethearts still need exercise, despite the presence of a mad man out there." Plus, he refused to hide in his own home and knew Parker felt the same. Even if he did lock her up, she'd find a way to escape and find herself in deeper danger. It was best if they went on as usual with him staying close by her side.

"Good. I look forward to the peacefulness of our evening ride." She took the reins and led her horse from the barn.

Colt followed and swung onto the saddle.

The setting sun kissed the top of Parker's dark head with gold, painting her arms with a rosy glow. She was still the most beautiful woman he'd ever seen, and he was still a sucker for her. Six months apart had done nothing to dull his feelings. Realizing he still loved her more than life itself was a knife to the gut.

He led the way, his mind whirling. He wanted to take a chance on her again—accept her apology and talk about what happened until he understood why she hadn't chosen him. How could he bring up the subject when the dread of rejection made him too much a coward? It was easier to be shot at yesterday than broach the subject with her.

Parker was uncharacteristically quiet on the ride which told him more than anything about how worried she was. If he could take away her fear, he would.

Please, God, don't let me fail her. If he did, he'd no longer feel as if he had a purpose. Everything he wanted in life would mean nothing.

"Do you like working on the Rocking W?" She asked, pulling her horse alongside him.

"Sure."

"Don't you want something more?"

He shot her a glance. "I want my own cattle ranch."

"What's stopping you?"

"Money, mostly. Land is expensive." Thankfully, his bank account grew every payday since his living expenses were few.

"Why not get a loan or find an investor?"

"Why pay something back with interest?"

She shrugged. "I'd invest in your ranch."

He pulled on the reins, halting his horse. "Why?"

She tilted her head. "Because I believe in you, Colton. I always have."

Reaching over, he gripped the horse's bit and pulled her closer. "Then why did you choose money over me?" He really didn't want to have this conversation, but they needed to in order for him to heal and move on. Tears brimmed in her eyes. "My father was so adamant. No matter how much I cried, he wouldn't be deterred. He said someday I'd understand. I still don't know why, but I trusted him. I'm so sorry." She ducked her head.

He stared at her through the growing darkness. Suppressing the many words that would cut deep, he managed to murmur, "Your father had to have said something to explain his reasoning."

"Nothing that he said made sense."

"What did he say?"

She met his eyes. "That it was too dangerous for me to continue seeing you. Dangerous for me, you, my parents… and after that he gave me one last warning. If I should continue on my path to marry you, I would lose everything."

"Everything? "What does that mean?"

"Looking back, it didn't have anything to do with money. I think he was being threatened, and that's why he made the demand. By the time I started believing this was his reason, you were gone."

His heart constricted. "You could have come to me."

"I was too embarrassed, and then trouble came. Doesn't it mean anything that you're the one I ran to?" Tears ran down her cheeks, glistening in the starlight.

It meant she needed help and thought he could rescue her. Colt might not be the right person for her to have chosen for the role, but he'd do everything in his power to meet her expectations. He ran his hand along her long tresses and pulled her face close for a kiss. For tonight, for a moment, he'd forget all that had transpired between them and hold onto a glimmer of hope for a future together.

Her lips rounded, and her soft breath washed over his face before he claimed his lips. The horses shifted under them, huffing and stomping their feet.

Colt pulled Parker into his lap. She wrapped her arms around his neck as he deepened the kiss.

Call him a fool, but he wanted, no needed, to give this woman another chance with his heart. But not until after the threat of death was behind them. Until then, he'd do his best to keep his distance and focus on keeping her alive. The thought of these soft lips so close was too much to resist. Everything he'd been holding back broke through into this kiss.

Chapter Thirteen

Coming to the Rocking W had been the best decision Parker had made in a very long time. It was probably her imagination, but she swore her lips still tingled from the horseback kiss from the night before. She hugged the bedsheet to her chest and smiled. Colt was going to forgive her for her stupidity. Things were going to be just fine between them. Somehow, she'd find a way to acquire the money for his cattle ranch. The hard part would be convincing him to accept the gift, or to consider it a loan without interest, if that made him feel better.

A sharp knock on her door propelled her from the bed. They were expecting a group of kids out of school for the summer for riding lessons and a cookout, both of which Parker was to help with. The riding lessons, yes. The cooking over an open fire, not so much.

"Coming. Sorry!" She sprinted for the bathroom, took a quick shower, threw on her jeans and cowboy boots, fed Tuxedo, then rushed out the door. Twenty minutes had to be a record for her.

She skidded to a halt at the sight of a white sheet of paper tacked to the post of her porch. With trembling hands, she yanked it free and read,

Get the cowboy to back off or he dies.

A warning for her to stay away from Colt

She glanced toward Colt's house. Should she show him the note? What could he do?

The killer had to be watching them. He had to have seen them in the woods last night. But why would he worry about her relationship with Colt? Not that there was a relationship exactly, but even if there were, what did it matter?

The clanging of the cowbell signaling breakfast pulled her attention back. She'd show Colt the note later. Shoving it into her pocket, she made a dash for the main house. The day promised to be a busy one that would keep her mind too occupied to dwell on all the unanswered questions, and she didn't want to distract either of them from their work.

Colt glanced up from the table when she entered, a question in his eyes. He always knew when something was on her mind.

Parker ducked her head and filled her plate with eggs and bacon before pasting on a smile and taking a seat at the table as far away from him as she could. Ignoring the frown that had replaced his questioning look, she ate as fast as she could, then excused herself, mumbling that she had some things to do at home before the guests arrived.

The pounding of hammers from those working on the barn accompanied her walk to her house. She entered and slammed the door, locking it behind her. If she didn't compose herself before seeing Colt again, he'd get too suspicious and demand she tell him what was on her mind. Parker was becoming a very bad liar.

Parker took a photo of the warning with her phone and sent it to the sheriff's department via text. She would still have to tell Colt, but at least she'd already done what he'd tell her to do.

A sharp rap sounded on her door.

She clasped a hand over her mouth, relaxing only when Colt peered through her window. Darn. She wouldn't be able to wait before alerting him to the note. "Good morning." She opened the door and offered a weak smile.

"Is it?" A muscle ticked in his jaw. "Mind telling me what has you more skittish than a yearling surrounded by coyotes?"

She sighed and pulled the wrinkled note from her pocket and handed it to him. "I was going to show you after the guests left. I've already texted a copy to the sheriff."

He grunted and read the note. "Did you think you were protecting me by not sharing this right away?"

"With all the kids coming, I didn't want to interfere with your work, so I put off telling you. It doesn't make sense that this person wants you out of the picture." She crossed her arms. "I know you well enough to know you won't run screaming into the night because of a warning."

"That's right." He glanced around the room. "I think it best that you move into the main house for a while. You're too easy to get to here."

"Would you move into the house?" She raised her brows, knowing the answer before he replied. "This note threatens you, not me. I still have a month before he comes for me."

His face darkened. "You make me crazy, Parker.

Of course, I won't hide in the main house. I'm not defenseless."

"Like a woman, you mean?" She marched up the stairs and retrieved her gun from the nightstand. "I'm not defenseless either," she said, returning downstairs.

"God help us."

The sound of tires crunching gravel alerted them that the guests had arrived.

"I'm going to have Maverick cover for me today so I can stay close to you." Colt turned to the door.

"That will just make things worse, Colt. Shouldn't we at least humor the guy…for now? What if your presence with the children puts them in danger? A killer might not stop at going through them to get to you. That's not the kind of memory you want these children to have of the ranch. Maverick is capable of helping me with the children."

He studied her face for a minute, then glanced back at the note. "You're right. I'll have to watch you from a distance. For now."

~

Colt hated that Parker made sense. While he trusted any of the ranch hands with her life, and his, he still felt better being the one by her side. "Let's get this day over with." He stepped onto the porch and scanned the area for anything or anyone that set his nerves tingling. Not finding anything, he led her to the front of the house and put her into the capable hands of Maverick. In a low voice, he filled the man in on the note.

"No worries. I'll keep her safe." The burn scar on Maverick's neck and lower jaw reddened. "If she's going to pack that gun, she should at least pull her shirt down to hide it." He motioned to where her shirt got caught on the weapon in her waistband. "Does she even know how to use a gun?"

"Yes." Colt had taught her himself. He tugged Parker's shirt over the gun, then marched to the barn construction despite everything in him wanting to stay with her and the kids. He'd have to be content to share the cookout with them and pray nothing happened.

After making sure the construction moved along on schedule, he entered the kitchen to check on whether the women had what they needed to feed the group.

"Hot dogs galore," Mrs. White said.

"And chips, the makings for s'mores, and chocolate drinks." Marilyn smiled. "Everything needed to send the kids home hyped-up on sugar. The local dry cleaner donated wire clothes hangers for them to toast their hot dogs and marshmallows on."

"Looks like you two have everything covered." Dylan had been smart enough from day one to hire people who didn't need micro-managing. Colt hoped to be the same type of ranch owner someday.

Back outside, he stood on the deck and stared toward the corral where the two tamest mares waited for rowdy riders to climb into the saddle. Parker gripped the reins of one horse, Maverick the other.

With things running as smoothly as they were, Colt felt as useless as Parker's kitten that watched him from the window of her house. When Dylan had asked him to be the foreman, he'd jumped at the chance. Turned out, Colt had done his job so well he occasionally had too much free time.

Another set of tires crunched in front of the house. Colt went to greet the new arrival, not surprised to see a squad car. "Deputy Hudson." He offered his hand for a shake.

The deputy grinned and returned the shake. "We sure are out here a lot since this ranch went into business." He glanced around. "Happens with isolation, I guess. Things are shaping up just fine."

"Thanks."

"You got another note?"

Colt nodded and fished it from his pocket. "Parker found it on her porch. Same as the others."

Hudson held out a bag for Colt to drop it into. "Tell her to stop touching them. The fewer prints, the better. It might not be a bad idea to put a camera on her porch, somewhere out of sight. Do it without being seen. We might catch a glimpse of this culprit."

Colt couldn't believe he didn't think of that himself. "There are some unused cameras in storage. I'll take care of that tonight." After everyone had gone to bed.

"Probably a good idea to have cameras on all the buildings. What about the main house? Did you check the cameras on the porch?"

"No. I'll get the code from Mr. Wyatt and do that tonight."

Hudson nodded. "I'll send this to the lab. Give Dylan my regards. Have a good day." He climbed back into his car and turned around, leaving a light plume of dust behind him.

Now having anything to do, Colt headed for the metal building used as storage. Unlocking the padlock on the door, he stepped inside and pulled the chain over his head to turn on the light.

Metal shelves lined the walls of the twenty-by-twenty room. Labels told anyone searching what each shelf held—thanks to Mrs. White's impeccable organization.

The door slammed shut casting him into total darkness.

"Hey, I'm in here." Sweat immediately beaded on his upper lip. He held his breath. Was he going to have a heart attack? "Hello?" His shirt stuck to his back. The oxygen levels in the storage shed were low. He was definitely going to die without the chance to tell Parker how he still felt about her.

Hands outstretched, he made his way to the door and pounded on it with both fists. His breathing became labored, and his fists ached from the pounding.

Stop. Breathe. Think.

He bent over, planting his hands on his knees and counted to ten. This wasn't a battle in the Middle East. He wasn't trapped underground after a bad mission. *I'm on the ranch surrounded by people. Someone will notice I'm gone. Someone will hear me.*" His phone. He slid it from his pocket. *Please find me a signal in the shed.*

He held the phone as high as he could trying to get enough bars to send a text at least. There. He sent Parker a text for help, telling her where he was. Now, he had to wait. In the dark. Alone. He slid to the floor.

He didn't know how long it took, just that it wasn't as long as it seemed before he heard Parker's voice. "Colton?"

"I'm here." He bolted to his feet.

"The padlock is locked."

"I'll slip the key under the door." He forced the key through the tiny sliver that let in just enough light to keep him from having slipped into madness.

A few seconds later, the doors swung open, and he rushed out. He exhaled heavily, then took a deep breath. "Thank you."

"You're all sweaty. Are you okay? I remember you being afraid of the dark." Concern covered her face.

"I'm not afraid of the dark." He glowered. "I don't like enclosed spaces."

"Okay? Are you fine?"

"I am now. Thank you. Someone locked me in."

"That's obvious."

"Parker—" He put his hands on her shoulders. She needed to comprehend what he was telling her. "That means the person we're looking for, the one leaving you notes, is here on the ranch. Today.

"He's close."

Chapter Fourteen

A box of security cameras in one hand and the necessary tools in the other, Colt toed off his boots and stepped onto Parker's front porch. Hopefully, he could get the job done and be gone without waking or frightening her.

He'd recently got the code to the main house cameras and also wanted to spend time going through them while the rest of the house slept. Daybreak brought work and its own demands. Putting off tasks to do later didn't work well on a ranch. He'd get through the day on a couple of hours sleep and multiple cups of coffee, if that's what it took to catch the man terrorizing Parker.

Colt retrieved the stepstool he'd sat on earlier and climbed up to install a camera. He'd already put one on his house and also on the empty house number two. After this, he'd head to Dylan's office.

Camera installed, he glanced down to make sure he put his foot solidly on the next rung and almost stepped on Tuxedo. The kitten stared up at him with big yellow eyes. "Hey, buddy. How did you get out?" He lifted his gaze to a grinning, tousle-headed Parker.

"We've been watching you. Good idea. Maybe

we'll catch this person."

"Hopefully. I wanted to keep this low-key."

"Do you think he's watching?" She picked up the kitten and glanced around.

"Anything is possible. I'm getting ready to look at footage from the main house camera. Want to join me?"

Her smile widened. "Sure. I'll bring coffee." She turned and carried the kitten into the house.

What prompted him to invite her? She'd be a distraction. Especially with the mussed-up hair and wrinkled pajamas. Lord, have her get dressed. Parker had never been one to think about how her clothes affected someone. She simply got...dressed. Which usually meant she looked awesome. But something about cotton shorts and a tank top instead of silky pajamas did more to his heart rate.

He tossed the tools in the box with the leftover cameras and returned them to his house before waiting on the back deck for Parker. She hadn't changed her clothes and held a coffee cup in each hand.

"What's wrong?" She peered up at him.

"Nothing." The problem was his, not hers. Spending so much time with her messed with his head...and his heart. Colt unlocked the back door to the kitchen, waved for Parker to go ahead of him, then stepped inside and locked the door. He put a finger to his lips, signaling her to be quiet.

When she nodded, he took the cup she offered him and led the way to the office. He waited to turn on the light until he had closed the door. Waking up Mrs. White would lead to a lot of questions he'd rather leave for later in the day. Already the lack of sleep was catching up to him.

He sat in Dylan's office chair and logged in while Parker pulled up an extra chair. Once he was into the security app, he typed in the code Dylan had texted him. Several screens came up, including the one from the newly installed camera on Parker's porch.

So, it worked. Great. He'd never called himself an electrician. Colt typed in the date she'd received the first note. The filmed footage popped onto the screen.

"There." Parker pointed at a man in a dark hoodie.

The man placed the rose and note on the banister, keeping his head down, and backed out of sight of the camera. Either he'd suspected there were cameras, or he'd scoped the place out beforehand.

"Do you recognize him?" Parker's breath tickled Colt's cheek.

"No. He could be any man in Misty Hollow or on the Rocking W." Of course, none of the ranch hands would dare harass a woman in this way. He'd bet his life on that. "I'm going to put a camera facing away from your house and one on the back. We need to get a glimpse of this man's face."

"Before now, I'd have said that might be overkill, but you go ahead and string the cameras like Christmas lights if you want to." She plopped back into her seat. "I still don't understand why he's after me. We're getting close to figuring out why my father was killed, and my mother since she was him, but why me? I had nothing to do with the construction company."

"It has to do with the note where he said he'd wanted to marry you." Since Parker had no idea who the man was, that note frightened Colt the most. It showed a truly disturbed mind.

Her brow furrowed. "Seriously, other than you,

I've not been in any long-term relationships, and didn't date much. College took up a lot of my time, then living on my own…not that I really needed the money. Mom and Dad took care of me, but if someone wanted to marry me, wouldn't I know?" She shook her head. "I'm rambling again."

"It's fine. You're nervous."

"That's an understatement, Colton. If it's okay with you, if I'm not needed in the kitchen or elsewhere today, I'm going to spend some more time going through the boxes in my house and finishing my father's journal. There's something there that will tell us who this man is. I know it."

"Let's consider combing through those boxes your job for now." She would be safer inside her house than anywhere other than the main house. "Keep the door locked, and don't open it unless you know the person."

"What if I know the person and he's the killer?" She arched a brow. "He wanted to marry me after all. I have to know him."

That made better sense than anything else. "You're right. It isn't going to be that simple."

~

The stupid cameras didn't bother him. He'd accomplished his mission despite them before. All it took was a well-covered face, a shuffling walk, a hunched back—all things that didn't look like him.

Staying in the shadows and out of sight of the camera, he set a small white jeweler's box on Parker's porch railing, then slipped away. Morning would come early, and they expected him back on the barn roof. His time on the ranch was coming to an end. The closer Parker and the cowboy got to discovering his identity, the less time he had. Plus, he needed to follow through on his threat. Parker wasn't keeping the cowboy at bay in the slightest.

Locking Dawson up in the shed should've been warning enough. After he overheard a couple of the ranch hands talking about what they'd brought back from the Middle East with them, finding out Dawson had a fear of closed-in spaces had given Mark the perfect tool. Only, it hadn't worked at keeping him and Parker apart.

Mark would have to step up his game before the deadline.

Glancing around to make sure no one watched him, he headed for the woods. He'd found the cameras in the trees on his first night. The red light blinking from the branches of a pine tree was a dead giveaway.

Maybe not all who roamed the night were as wise and observant as he was. In fact, he knew they weren't. Enjoy the gift, Parker.

Out of range of the cameras, he settled back to wait for the right time to leave another message.

~

"Stop." Colt put a hand in front of Parker.

"Why?"

"There's a box on your porch."

Her heart leaped into her throat. Could they have caught the culprit on camera so soon? "Go back and check the laptop."

He cut her a sideways look. "And leave you alone? Not a chance. We aren't opening that box without gloves. Hudson told me to be more careful."

"The only ones I have are pink leopard print that I use for cleaning." She couldn't help but grin at the thought of Colt wearing them.

"Come on. I have some in my house." He hurried her to his place where he retrieved some thin latex gloves. Handing her a pair, he led her back home.

Parker grabbed the white box before he could and lifted the lid. She gasped and dropped it. A severed finger rolled a few inches across her porch. Nausea roiled in her stomach.

Colt sprang into action and grabbed the appendage, then dropped it back into the box. "There's a business card." He pulled it from the box and handed it to her.

"Oh." She swallowed against the sourness rising in her throat. "It's the private investigator's card. Is this his finger?"

"If I had to make a guess, but let me get a hold of the sheriff's office. Someone needs to check on the man." Colt replaced the box on the railing, pulled his cell phone from his pocket, and left a message with the deputy on duty. He hung up and returned his attention to Parker. "They'll get back to us after they check on him."

"He's in Little Rock." She wrapped her arms around her waist, chilled despite it being a summer evening.

"Let's go inside." Leaving the box where he'd set it, he held out his hand. "Key."

She dropped it into his palm, more than happy to let him take control. Once inside, she rushed to the bathroom and splashed cold water on her face.

"Do you want me to make coffee?" Colt called out.

"Yes, thank you. I won't be able to sleep until I find out what happened to Mr. Watson." His name had made her smile when she'd hired him, thinking of

Sherlock, but now her heart filled with dread at what might have happened to him.

Coffee made, they sat at her table for two. Parker spent more time staring into her cup than she did drinking it. How long until the sheriff's department got back to them? "How will they find him?"

"The PI? Most likely, the department here will contact LRPD who will then send someone out to check on the man." He reached over and put his hand over hers. "We wait, Parker. They'll let us know."

An hour later, a knock sounded at the door. Colt motioned for her to remain seated. "It's Sheriff Westbrook." He opened the door and let him in.

Parker jumped to her feet. "Well?"

"Mr. Miller was found shot dead in his bed and missing a finger. I'm going to assume the missing finger is in the box on your porch." Sheriff Westbrook's features hardened. "Let's take a look at the camera footage, Colt."

Parker stared over the two mens' shoulders at nothing. Since the camera faced her front door, the person who left the box had been able to do so without stepping foot on the porch. "Maybe my idea of a string of cameras isn't such a bad idea."

"We definitely need more." Colt closed the laptop. "What now, Sheriff?"

"The two of you try to get some sleep. I'd prefer it if you both moved into the main house or at least Parker. You could move back to the bunkhouse until this is over. Anywhere the two of you aren't alone."

They headed back outside.

A shot rang out.

Colt wrapped his arms around Parker and dove off

the deck. They landed in the bushes, her on top of him.

"Stay down," the sheriff ordered. "Shot fired from the woods. I'm going after him."

Colt rolled Parker off him. "Not alone, sir." He started to get to his feet.

"It's the two of you he's after. Call for backup and do as I say." Weapon in hand, the sheriff raced for the trees.

Chapter Fifteen

For the last two days, Parker had dug through boxes and read her father's journal. Both jobs were almost complete. With every box she opened, every line she read, she felt one step closer to discovering the identity of the man who had killed her parents.

The sheriff hadn't found more than footprints and tire tracks when he'd gone after the shooter the other night. If the authorities couldn't catch the man, what made Parker think she could? Oh, sure, she felt as if she'd come a long way from the spoiled, little rich girl, but she was still no crime fighter.

Parker lay in the bed in the main house and stared at the ceiling. She reached over to pet Tuxedo, sitting upright when her hand encountered nothing but mattress.

Oh, no. Colt had told her the cat had to stay in her room. According to Colt, the boss didn't allow animals in the house.

She padded barefoot around the second floor of the house. "Here, kitty, kitty." Where was that darn cat?

The soft murmurs of Mrs. White drifted up the stairs. Parker headed for the kitchen.

The cook knelt next to a bowl of milk the kitten had her head in, lapping as if she'd never been fed. "You are a sweetie."

"Thank you for finding her before someone who has an aversion to cats did." Parker smiled.

"Oh, she found me and started begging like you wouldn't believe." Mrs. White rose to her feet.

"I believe it, and she's actually a he. A sweet little boy that always wants to eat." Parker headed for coffee, relieved to see a fresh pot. "Have you seen Colt this morning?"

"He's in the office."

Parker paused, reaching for a cup. "Did he see Tuxedo?"

"Yep. That man can scowl. But I gave him a slice of apple pie, a cup of coffee, and told him to take his surly attitude somewhere else. I can invite anyone into my kitchen I want, and if he doesn't like it, he can take it up with the boss when he returns."

"Only you could get away with talking to him like that." Parker laughed.

"Not just me." She returned Parker's smile. "You could get him to do almost anything. He might grumble, but he'd do it all the same."

She liked to think so. Despite the steps they'd made repairing their relationship, they still had a long way to go. "Anything I can help you with?"

"Finished going through your father's things?"

"No."

"Then, no, I don't need you. Marilyn and I can handle things. We've another group of kids showing up tomorrow. I'll need you then. Focus on what's important right now, and that's finding out who killed your parents."

Parker gave her an impulsive hug. "Thank you." She finished fixing her coffee, scooped up Tuxedo, and headed home to do some more digging after a quick shower.

Her steps slowed as she approached her front door. Not seeing any notes or boxes, the tension left her shoulders, and she unlocked her front door, making sure to bolt it behind her once she stepped inside.

"Go keep watch, you little scamp." She set Tuxedo on the floor and went to get ready for the day.

First thing after her shower, she sat at the table with a fresh cup of coffee beside her and finished the journal. No more secret messages between glued pages appeared, but the last page did speak a lot about her father's suspicions regarding someone stealing from the company.

Another page told of cutting corners on building projects. A man had died as a result when a poorly constructed roof didn't hold and caved in on the poor man.

Parker closed the journal. So her father had been accused of cutting corners. As a result, he would've started investigating in order to clear his name. The person responsible had killed him, and now he came after Parker. Why her? Again, she had nothing to do with her father's business.

What did she have that someone would want? Money. The only thing she had was money, and lots of it. Could it be that simple? Did this man want the money he'd try to achieve by ill-gotten gains and, having failed, he wanted Parker to give it to him? Then why not ask?

She sighed and finished her coffee while staring out the window at the workers. One of the construction crew could very well be the man who killed her family. What would she do if she discovered who?

She liked to believe she'd do the right thing and alert the sheriff rather than foolishly confront the man. But, Parker didn't always do the smartest thing. She was learning, though. This time, rushing ahead without thinking things through could get her and someone else killed.

Coffee cup empty, she moved to the floor and opened the last of her father's boxes. A few files of receipts sat on top waiting for the next tax season. Newspapers lay underneath. Parker removed them and started flipping through, stopping only when an article referred to her father or Wells Construction.

Bingo. A full-page article complete with a clear black and white photograph that showed her father and his staff during the ribbon-cutting ceremony of an office complex. The very complex that later fell apart, killing a man.

Parker peered closer. She recognized one of the men in the photo. Her gaze darted to the window. The man now sat on the roof of the barn.

Clutching the newspaper, she dashed from her house in search of Colt.

~

Mark narrowed his eyes as Parker darted across the lawn. Her furtive glance his way told him all he needed to know. She recognized him.

He scurried down the ladder and made a beeline for his truck. Minutes later, he spun gravel speeding away from the ranch. He'd have to check out of the motel and find another place to hole up until he made his final confrontation.

Misty Hollow would be swarming with law enforcement and cowboys—neither of which he was ready to face yet.

How had she found out? They'd never met each other face-to-face. Her father's refusal to introduce him to his daughter had kept that from happening. Then the accusation had come, and Mark had to kill the man. The wife had just been collateral damage.

Knowing Parker would never agree to date him once she found out, he refrained from approaching her. She'd been in a time of mourning. No, the only way he could get the money he felt was due him was to convince her to give it to him. Then, he'd kill her—in that order.

His knuckles whitened on the steering wheel as he took the mountain curves too sharply. Slow down, man, before you go over the cliff.

There'd been no time for her to sound the alarm yet. Mark knew the drill. First, she'd have to talk to the foreman, then they'd call the sheriff. Then, the law would show up at the ranch, but he would be nowhere around. He'd planned everything down to the tiniest detail with a plan A and a plan B. A wiseman always knew his next move.

~

Colt sprang into action after scanning the newspaper article. "Are there more in the box?"

"Yes."

"I want to go through them once we alert the sheriff." He placed the call. The sheriff said he'd be there in twenty minutes.

Back at Parker's house, Colt dug through the papers until he found the last article written about the embezzlement—the one referring to the accident her parents had died in. "Your father named Mark Cooper as the embezzler, except Cooper goes by Collins now." Why hadn't this shown up in his background check? "I need to make another call." He dialed the construction company building the barn.

Parker nodded and dropped to the sofa.

"Hey, Townsend, did you ever get all the background checks back on your workers?"

"Sure, but I haven't gone through them. The barn is almost finished, so I didn't see the rush."

"One of the men, Collins, is actually Mark Cooper, an embezzler and murderer. This isn't going to look good for your business, Mr. Townsend." His hand tightened around his phone.

"You threatening me?"

"No, just letting you know what happens when a man doesn't do his job properly. I want an inspector, at your expense, here today to go over the work on the barn. I can't have shoddy work, which Collins is known for."

"You got it." Townsend hung up.

"What do we do now?" Parker hugged a throw pillow to her chest.

"Wait for the sheriff." He went to the window and stared out. "Did you see Collins on your way to the house?"

"He was on the barn roof."

"Well, he isn't there now." He fled most likely. "The sheriff's here." He grabbed the newspapers from where he'd set them on the desk and led the way to the front porch.

Sheriff Westbrook removed his hat as he approached the house. "Sounds like we're finally getting somewhere."

"Yes, sir." Colt handed him the articles. "We know the identity and the motive. I don't think Collins is on the ranch anymore."

"That would make it too easy." The sheriff tucked the newspapers under his arm. "The man will be desperate now. The two of you need to be more vigilant than ever. If you see him, do not engage him. Call the department. We don't need any more casualties." His gaze flicked to Parker. "You holding up?"

She nodded. "Yup, I'm determined to see this through to the end, so I can resume my life."

Did that mean she'd be leaving the ranch? Colt frowned. Isn't that what he'd wanted from the moment he set eyes on her again?

Hearing those words confused him. What did they mean? Was he just a temporary fix?.

"Hopefully, it won't be long now," the sheriff said.

"No longer than three more weeks anyway." The reminder of the deadline brought Colt back to the conversation.

"We'll have this done by then." He guaranteed. No way would he let the deadline approach for Mark to come for Parker. Not while he still breathed. Once the man was behind bars, Colt would ask her to stay and build the cattle ranch with him. He'd set aside the pain of her former rejection. She was here now. That's all that mattered to him. The past could stay in the past. He put an arm around her shoulder and pulled her to his side. "I won't let her out of my sight, Sheriff. That, I can promise."

"Good." The sheriff nodded. "Remember there's a target on your back, too. This man doesn't like the two of you together, most likely because it makes it harder for him to gain access to Parker. He won't hesitate to get rid of you to apprehend her."

"I know." Colt squared his shoulders. "It won't be easy for Collins."

The sheriff's mouth quirked. "Don't reckon it will. I'll put an APB out on him. What kind of vehicle does he drive?"

"An older model, navy-blue Chevy with a busted right taillight. Empty gun rack in the window." Colt liked to pride himself on his attention to detail, but he wished he'd caught on to Collins weeks ago.

That mistake could cost Parker her life.

Chapter Sixteen

Mark hadn't been spotted in days. The ranch hands worked double time to prepare for the return of the Wyatt family, and now the moment arrived.

Parker stood in front of the house with the rest of the staff and wiped sweaty palms down her jeans. Colt had told the boss about the recent trouble, but now that he was returning with his wife and kids, would he order Parker to leave? He might consider the danger too great for her to stay.

"Relax." Colt gave her hand a quick squeeze. "Everyone Dylan hires has a past—some trouble that haunts them." Another squeeze, and he headed down the steps to welcome the boss home.

A beautiful blond woman, her arms around two dark-haired boys, smiled and strolled toward the house. Her husband, a man standing well over six feet, shook hands with Colt.

"Hi, I'm Dani, and these two rascals are Eric and Derrick." The woman smiled and told the boys to take their bags to their rooms. "And that gorgeous hunk of flesh is Cyclone." She pointed past her husband to the inky black stallion being backed from a horse trailer. "His new wives are coming up the road now."

"Successful trip." Parker smiled, glad of the woman's welcoming nature.

"Very." Her shrewd gaze returned to Parker. "Heard you've had some trouble. Mind walking with me?"

Oh, no. This was it. Instead of telling her himself to leave, the boss would have his wife do it. "Sure." Parker forced her tone to remain light as she fell into step with Dani.

So many denials rose to her lips only to be tamped down. The trouble she'd brought with her was not her fault, but it still lay on her shoulders if someone was harmed.

As they walked, Dani told her of the troubles she'd brought to the ranch, starting with a crime boss tracking her to Misty Hollow, mistaking her twin sister for her, then a new evil a few months later after she started working on the ranch. "We're a bunch of misfits—all running from something. There's no better place to be, Parker."

"You aren't going to send me away?"

She laughed. "Of course not."

"But...the boys."

"They'll balk at some temporary restrictions on their time, but we'll keep them so busy they won't cause much of a ruckus. Show me your house. I haven't seen them finished."

"Mine is messy with my father's boxes, but you'll get the general idea."

"If you're finished with the boxes, we can have them carted away. I'm sure the sheriff's office would hold on to them as evidence." Her smile widened. "Yes, Colt has told us everything. I think he has, anyway."

"I'm sure he has." Colt's work ethic would make him very transparent. "I'll be glad to get rid of them." All she wanted to keep was her father's journal. She also needed to pack up the family home, keep what she wanted of her mother's, and sell the rest. Even if she didn't stay at the ranch once Mark was caught, she couldn't move back there. It held too many memories. She'd sell both it and her apartment. Start fresh somewhere else if Colt didn't want her.

She unlocked her front door and stepped aside for Dani to enter.

"How cute." Dani strolled through the small space, weaving in and out of the boxes. "Looks comfortable enough."

"It is."

"I'm glad to see there are cameras installed." She didn't miss much.

"Colt installed them at the sheriff's suggestion." Parker scooped Tuxedo from the counter. "One of Mark Collins' gifts. This one I kept."

"Can't say as I blame you. He's adorable. Keep your door locked, or the twins will be in here after him." She turned to face Parker. "I have one suggestion."

"Okay." Her nerves twanged.

"Please don't be alone with the boys. It isn't personal. When my trouble came after me, the boys were caught in the middle."

She nodded. "I understand and promise not to be alone with them. Usually, I'm in the house or helping with a group of children guests. If not at one of those places, I'm in my house reading."

"Thank you for understanding." She rubbed her

hands together. "So, make us some coffee and tell me about you and Colt."

"What makes you think there's anything to tell?" Parker's face heated.

"You were holding hands when we pulled up."

Parker put a coffee pod in the maker. "He was reassuring me that I wouldn't be kicked off the ranch."

"But—"

"We used to be engaged." She took a deep breath. "My father told me he'd disown me if I married Colt, that it was too dangerous for either of us. I don't think Colt ever forgave me for not choosing him over my family."

Dani shrugged. "You're here now."

"Because I didn't know who else to go to for help." She stared at the dark liquid dripping into the cup she'd placed under the spout. "He almost refused to help me."

"Men often let their pride get in the way." Dani sat at the small kitchen table. Tuxedo jumped into her lap. "Don't worry about being asked to leave. Dylan would never turn you away. This ranch was built for the wounded."

"That's what Colt said." She handed Dani the cup of coffee and some packets of cream and sugar before putting in another pod for herself. "Since I have nowhere else to go other than my parents' empty house, I appreciate being able to stay. There's safety in numbers, so they say." She took her cup and sat across from the other woman. "Your mother is Marilyn?"

"Yep."

"She's something. Your mother and Mrs. White have started carrying guns in their apron pockets."

"They did the same when I was in trouble." She laughed and stirred sugar into her coffee. "Thankfully, neither of them had a need to use them." She sobered. "The man after me came on a campout. Me and the boys got away from him by escaping into the woods. Fortunately, the twins know this mountain like the pages of their favorite book."

Parker didn't know the lay of the land. If she was lured away from the ranch, she'd be at a loss, especially if it involved the forest. Give her city streets any day. The streets and a handful of cash. She could buy the help she needed, find a place to hide—all things she'd considered if the danger reached those on the ranch.

~

"He's a beauty." Colt ran his hands down the horse's flanks. "He's going to sire some winners."

"I hope so." Dylan smiled. "Thanks for holding down the fort. The tiny houses and the barn look great." He motioned his head to where Townsend climbed around on the roof. "What's he doing?"

"Making sure Collins did the job he was paid to do. After finding out Townsend hadn't pushed through with the background checks, I told him he had to inspect the work personally before any further work was done."

"I'd have done the same. We don't want the place falling apart and injuring someone or one of the horses." He led Cyclone to the temporary barn. "Anything else I need to know since we last emailed?"

"Nope. The sheriff put an APB out on Collins and his truck. There's been no sign of the man since we found out his identity. The clerk at the motel said he hasn't seen him in a few days. I don't think he's gone for good, though. The man is biding his time."

Dylan nodded. "It won't be easy for him to get back on the ranch. Not with everyone on high alert."

"No, but he's smart. He'll find a way."

"We'll catch him when he does." Dylan led the horse into an empty stall, then closed the door.

Colt certainly hoped so, before someone was injured or worse.

"Dad!" The twins barged into the barn.

Cyclone reared and snorted.

"Hush, before the horse hurts himself."

"Monster brought home a girlfriend. She's fat." Eric pointed.

Colt shared an amused look with Dylan. "I'll check it out." He followed the boys outside to see a very pregnant mutt staring up at him with soulful eyes. Monster wagged his tail. "Let's make her a bed in the barn, boys. There'll be puppies in a day or two."

"Yippee!" Derrick darted inside. By the time Colt entered, the new dog in his arms, a bed had been made in the corner out of old army blankets.

"This should be good. We'll make a fence out of sacks filled with hay to keep the puppies from wandering around," Eric said. "We don't want them to get stepped on."

"Nope." Colt laughed. "We don't want that." The anticipation of a batch of new puppies shoved aside the worry about Collins, even if for a little while. The normalcy of new life outshone the uncertainty of evil.

Parker and Dani headed his way. He hoped the two would become friends. Parker could use a good friend. A woman to vent to, share secrets with, confide in— whatever it was women talked about.

"What's this?" Dani stared down at the dog.

"A very pregnant visitor," Colt said.

"Oh, I want one." Parker bent and patted the dog's head.

"What are you going to do with a dog in a tiny house?" Colt tilted his head.

"I won't always live in that house."

The reminder that she'd leave once the threat of danger was past tore at him. He might not have decided whether he actually wanted to pursue a future with her, but he also didn't want her to leave. Colton Dawson was one confused cowboy. "You plan on returning home?"

She shook her head. "I'm going to sell that house. Make a fresh start." She straightened, her gaze meeting his. "Again, I'm thinking of staying in Misty Hollow."

The thought gave him joy.

"Let's get the new dog some food and water." Dylan shooed his family out of the barn, a knowing gleam in his eyes.

Colt didn't care. Let them speculate on his conversation with Parker.

"How would you feel about that?" Uncertainty flickered in her eyes.

"I don't know for sure. Glad, I think. What would you do?"

She shrugged. "Anything I want. My parents left me very well off. Maybe I'll form a charity. I've got time to think about what I want to do." A question formed in her eyes. She started to say something else, then ducked her head. "I'd best go see if I'm needed in the kitchen."

He wanted to tell her to stay on the ranch. But what

about when he left the Rocking W? This place wasn't his permanent home. Was he ready to ask her to go wherever he did? Rather than act on his thoughts, he turned back to the dog, making sure she was comfortable enough to welp her puppies. Then, not finding anything else that needed his immediate attention, he exited the barn and closed the door.

At supper that evening, the mood was high as everyone welcomed back the Wyatt family. The place might have run smoothly in their absence, but having the lead family back completed the circle.

Since the first day Dylan opened the doors to his fellow military heroes, whether emotionally or physically damaged, they'd been one big family willing to do anything for each other. Even face danger.

It was times like this that kept Colt dragging his feet on purchasing his own land and starting his own ranch. He'd miss the camaraderie of this place.

Tires crunched outside.

Every head in the dining room turned.

Seeing the sheriff's car, Dylan stood, motioning for Colt to go with him.

Sheriff Westbrook met them on the porch. "We found the truck. No sign of Collins."

Chapter Seventeen

After meeting Dani Wyatt and realizing she wouldn't be asked to leave the ranch, Parker headed for her tiny house the next morning to pack up the boxes the sheriff would send someone to collect. She glanced both ways before stepping onto the deck. Seeing Monster lying there, she relaxed. The dog would be on alert if someone was around who didn't live on the ranch.

At least that was Parker's reasoning. "Come with me, boy. I could use the company, and since I'm not supposed to be alone, you'll keep me from getting into trouble with Colt." Did the dog count as a guardian?

Her steps faltered at the sight of a shoebox next to her front door.

Monster's ears perked. A whine came from deep in his throat before he sprang forward and nosed the box.

With trembling fingers, Parker removed the lid. Lying inside on a dirty rag lay a squirming, whining, newborn puppy. "Oh, you poor thing." She scooped the puppy into her hand, keeping it wrapped in the rag. "Let's get you to your mommy." Then, she'd find Colt.

The gifts from Mark had to stop. This pup would've died if she hadn't discovered it by nightfall.

Colt reached her by the time she turned and stepped off her porch. "Why are you alone? Don't you listen to anyone, including the sheriff?"

"Monster is with me." She thrust out her hands. "Another gift. Obviously, Mark is smarter than the cameras."

His eyes widened as his face turned the color of a beet. He moved to her porch and studied the camera for a moment before waving his hand in front of it. Then, he dashed to the corner of the main house, Parker and Monster on his heels.

"Only the wire to the cameras has been cut." He stared toward the thick trees behind the house. "How is he getting close enough?"

"He has to have help, Colton. Someone on this ranch must be helping him."

"No. We trust them." He shook his head.

"There is no other explanation." She glanced toward the bunkhouse. "We need to talk to Dylan. First, let me return this baby."

Colt escorted her to the barn and waited while she placed the puppy back with its mother and four litter mates. "I still want one when they're old enough." Parker smiled and straightened. "A little girl."

"I'm sure that won't be a problem."

They found Dylan in his office. He listened with a stony face as they told him about finding the puppy. When Parker started to explain her suspicions about one of the ranch hands, he held up a hand to stop her. "Let's wait for the sheriff. I don't want to ruin my breakfast more than it already has been." He reached for his phone and made the call before heading for the dining room. "When is our next group of guests arriving?"

"Tomorrow," Colt said. "Should we cancel? There will be six twelve-year-olds, all boys wanting to learn some camping skills."

"Overnight?"

"No."

Dylan nodded. "No need to cancel, then. Collins always seems to come under the cover of darkness."

Parker couldn't shake the idea that one of the ranch hands was helping Mark. What the ranch needed was undercover deputies, not rowdy children. Once Mark was captured and locked up, then life could get back to normal on the ranch. She followed the men into the dining room. Again, she thought of leaving. If she did, the danger would follow her. Her gaze landed on Colt's strong back. But so would he—of that, she had no doubt. He'd committed to keeping her safe and wouldn't stop from doing so, even if it meant putting himself in harm's way.

The sheriff arrived toward the end of breakfast, and Parker followed him, Colt, and Dylan back to the ranch office. Arms crossed, she listened as Colt explained about her finding the pup and the cut wire.

When he finished, she interjected. "I think one of the ranch hands is helping Mark."

Dylan whipped to face her. "Impossible. I trust them all."

"Then you explain how he gets on and off this ranch." She arched a brow. "Because it is impossible, unless he has help. Someone willing to cut wires and steal puppies from a nursing mother. It has to be someone here, or Monster would've sounded the alarm."

Dylan shared a look with Colt. "But who? Willy has been here since day one. Maverick, Clay, Deacon, Ryder, and River almost as long."

"That leaves the more recent hires. Bill, Lincoln, and Darryl." Colt rubbed both hands roughly down his face. "Since Bill was killed a few months back, that leaves Lincoln and Darryl."

"How well do you know them?" Parker refused to sway from her idea. "What do you think, Sheriff?"

"I think you're on to something. Having someone helping him explains a lot."

"It's time for you to send us someone undercover." Parker hitched her chin.

Dylan frowned. "Is it? We're capable of keeping an eye on those two."

"I'm going to have to insist." She hated reverting back to the spoiled princess who made demands, but this was matter of life and death. "I'm putting my foot down."

Colt gave a sarcastic laugh. "There's the Parker I used to know. This isn't your ranch, Darlin'."

Sheriff Westbrook sighed. "She's right. I'm sending Buster. He isn't one of my deputies, but he's just as good, and we've used him before."

"Marilyn will be happy," Dylan said. "Okay. I'll go along with having another body on the ranch. We'll keep the reason between us."

"What about questioning the two men you suspect?" Parker's eyes darted from one man to the other. "Surely, you know them well enough to know whether they're lying about any of the questions you ask them."

"Maybe we should just let Parker handle this whole thing." Dylan looked amused by her obvious sarcasm. "She's thinking way ahead of the rest of us."

She shrugged. "I don't have as much to do as you two, which leaves me more time for my mind to spin." A flicker of pride went through her. They believed her—something that hadn't happened a lot in her past. Most of the time, any ideas she'd had were brushed aside as nonsense. These men were different.

Even when Colt didn't agree with her, he always weighed what she said.

On cue, Colt nodded. "Want me to fetch Lincoln and Darryl?"

~

"Yep," the sheriff replied. "Keep them separate. Parker, I'm going to ask you to remain in the kitchen with the other women. We don't want these men to suspect anything."

Her brow furrowed. "Okay, but I want to hear about everything when it's over." Her gaze shot to Colt.

"I'll fill you in." He felt better knowing she'd be out of the way while the men were questioned. If one of them became defensive, he didn't want her in the way.

"While you fetch them, I'll call Buster." The sheriff stepped into the hall.

"I'll go." Colt followed, then headed outside.

He located Lincoln forking hay in the barn and Darryl cleaning Daisy's hooves. "Boss wants to talk to you." He jerked his head toward the house.

"What for?" Lincoln glanced up. "We do something wrong?'

Colt shrugged. "He just told me to fetch you. I wouldn't keep him waiting if I were you."

Lincoln huffed, then leaned the shovel against the wall. "Does he want us both together?"

"No."

"Then, I'll go first. See you later, Darryl."

"Yep." The other man watched him leave, then returned to his work as if he didn't have a care in the world.

Maybe Parker was wrong after all. Colt followed Lincoln. After a few questions, it became clear the man had no idea what they were talking about. He even seemed angry that someone would threaten one of those on the ranch.

Colt left in search of Darryl. This time, he found him nursing a cup of coffee in the kitchen and laughing at something Mrs. White said. "Your turn."

Darryl drained his cup, set it in the sink, then followed Colt. "What's up?" He paled at seeing the sheriff in Dylan's office.

"Have a seat, Mr. Wilson." The sheriff motioned at an empty chair. "This won't take long. How well do you know Mark Collins?"

"The guy who worked with the construction crew? A bit. Had a few beers with him."

"Know anything about him?"

Darryl grinned. "He's got the hots for Parker Wells."

Colt exchanged a glance with Dylan. "He tell you that?"

"Yep. Oh." His eyes widened. "This about the cut security camera wire? I meant to repair that this morning. I'm sorry."

"You cut it?" The sheriff frowned.

"Yeah. Collins wanted to leave Parker a surprise

gift. He paid me a hundred bucks to help him do it without getting caught. Said it would ruin all the fun if it wasn't a surprise."

Colt wanted to strangle the idiot. "Are you aware that Collins is a suspect in a murder investigation? That he has made threats against Parker? Death threats?"

"No." Darryl's brows furrowed. "He said he liked her. I wouldn't have helped him if I'd known otherwise."

"How long have you been helping him?" The sheriff asked.

"Just a few times. I saw the chance to make an easy couple of bucks, but I didn't mean any harm."

"Done anything else that we aren't aware of that would allow Collins easy access to the ranch?" Dylan's eyes flashed.

"No, I swear. I only helped him onto the ranch a couple of times."

"Did you take the puppy out of the barn last night? Do you know where Collins is?"

"He moved out of the motel. I don't know where he went, and no I didn't move the puppy out of the barn." Again, he shook his head. "I did see him slip into the barn last night and then out, but didn't think he intended any harm."

"That's the problem, Darryl. You didn't think through any of this." Dylan stood from his chair. "Pack your things. You're fired. If I see you anywhere near the Rocking W, I'll have you arrested."

"But…"

"No buts. Your dismissal is effective immediately. I'll make sure you receive a decent referral so you can work on a different ranch. Colt, see this man off the

Rocking W."

"Yes, sir." Colt gripped Darryl's arm. "Let's go."

They passed Parker on their way through the kitchen.

"I'm sorry, ma'am. I meant no harm." He hung his head.

Her stricken gaze met Colt's. "Guess my idea worked."

"Guess it did. It won't be as easy for Collins to get close to you now." He prodded the man from the house.

Curious eyes followed them to the bunkhouse where Colt waited for Darryl to pack the few items he owned. "You're lucky the boss is giving you a referral."

"Yeah. I liked it here, but I'll find work again. The cowboy life is fading, and there are always ranches in need of good hands." He zipped his army-green duffel bag closed. "I'm grateful for the opportunity to work here."

"Maybe you'll use your head the next time." Colt led him to where the hired men parked their vehicles. "If you see Collins, don't alert him. Just call the sheriff. Can you do that?"

"It's the least I can do." He tossed his bag into the back seat of a beat-up sedan. "Nice knowing you, Colt."

"Yep." He wished he could say the same, but after knowing about the man's foolish escapades to make extra money, he'd lost all respect for him. He stood in the driveway as Darryl drove away from the ranch. Again, he felt incompetent at keeping Parker safe. How did he not suspect one of the ranch hands of helping Collins?

Because he'd trusted them, same as Dylan had. He'd trusted the wounded, the lost, and the ex-military men, assuming they all shared the same code of honor he did. That trust had led him to make a huge mistake. A mistake that could have killed Parker.

Chapter Eighteen

Colt bolted upright with a shout. Perspiration soaked the sheet under him. Another dream of him failing when his skills were needed most. Only this time the sightless eyes staring up at him were Parker's.

He swung his legs over the side of the bed and buried his face in his hands. The time was fast approaching when he'd see exactly how much he'd succeed or fail. *Please, God, don't let me fail.*

A glance at the clock spurred him into action. A cool shower helped him wake up and wash away the sweat, but it did little to dispel the fear rising in his throat. He thought he'd had a good grip on things until finding out about Darryl's idiocy—a man Colt had hired during Dylan's trip overseas. He tried to tell himself that everyone made mistakes. The man's references had been impeccable, and he'd met all the ranch requirements of needing a place to heal, but Colt's decision to hire the man could have resulted in something terrible happening to Parker.

With a sigh, he gave himself a mental shake. He needed to trust in himself and no one else. Colt had what it took to keep Parker safe. Right. Maybe if he said it enough, he'd start to believe it.

Dressed, he headed to the barn to move the female dog and her puppies to a place where they'd be safe from excited twelve-year-olds. Since the forecast called for rain, all survival-skill training would take place in the barn and under a tarp outside. The noon meal would be served in the main-house dining room.

If Colt had his way, he'd cancel the whole thing, but Dylan didn't see the need. If they were camping or horseback riding instead of fire building, water purifying, and cooking, he'd have rescheduled.

"Come on, girl. Let's move you into a back stall." He placed the puppies on a clean blanket and carried them to the farthest stall, knowing the mother would follow. Once he'd moved them safely out of harm's way, he led the horses to pasture before heading to breakfast. "You keep a good eye out, Monster." He patted the dog's head. The mutt probably missed the two security jobs Dylan had rented a few months back. Maybe if they still had them, Mark wouldn't have been able to slip onto the ranch as easily with or without help.

Yep, he'd make sure he had at least two dogs when he started his ranch.

"Good morning." Parker rushed down her porch steps and fell into step beside him. "I'd ask how you slept, but the dark circles under your eyes say it all. Bad dreams?"

"Yep."

"The same one you used to have?"

"Pretty much." He opened the kitchen door for her. "Ready for our group?"

"As ready as I can be knowing absolutely nothing about what you'll be teaching them."

He grinned. "Good thing you'll be there to learn."

"Right." She laughed. "I'll do my best to make sure none of the kiddos wander off. I am basically going to be a babysitter, right? That and a sous-chef."

"Yep, but they'll be preparing their own food."

They filled their plates with eggs and bacon before choosing their seats at the table. Colt went over the daily chore list with the other men as they ate. "Willy, stay close by in case I need your help with the skill class. The rest of you are on patrol and regular daily chores."

"We have a schedule," Maverick said, lowering his voice as he glanced at the twins sitting at the far end of the table. "The ranch is big, but we've come up with a grid that will work at covering the expanse."

"Be vigilant. We don't want a repeat of Bill." The man had been killed while on patrol trying to keep Dani's assailant from getting too close.

"As long as things go smoothly with everything else, there will be more than one of us patrolling on horseback." Maverick dug into his eggs.

Good. The men had everything under control. Still, the idea that Mark could still find a way to get to Parker ate at him. There was always a way if someone wanted something bad enough. And this man was obsessed with Parker—according to his threatening notes anyway. Colt reassured himself that the ranch was as safe as they could make it. Now he just had to believe it.

~

Parker cleared the table then stepped onto the front porch to wait for their guests. By the time she finished working at the ranch, once Mark was behind bars, she'd feel a lot more comfortable around kids than she had before arriving at the ranch to ask for Colt's help.

She leaned her elbows on the railing and stared down the long drive. White fences lined the dirt drive; horses grazed in corrals on each side of it. Such a marvelously beautiful place. If someone would have told her last year that she'd be living in a house the size of her bedroom and working on a ranch, she'd have told them they were insane. But she loved her new life— minus the danger, that is.

A dust plume let her know the bus carrying the days guests had turned onto the path. She knocked on the kitchen window to let the other two women know.

The twins barged outside, insistent they be there to greet the other kiddos. "After all, we're doing some of the training," Eric said, crossing his arms.

"Settle down, cowboy. Nobody said you couldn't be out here." Parker shook her head, then smiled as Colt strolled around the corner of the house as a fine mist fell from the dark clouds overhead.

He wiped his hands on the legs of his jeans. "Ready?"

"Yep!" Both boys yelled, their arms held high.

"Then, let's go." Colt led them to where six twelve-year-olds scampered from the bus.

Their teacher/chaperone for the day, Susan Snodgrass, shook Colt's hand. "Here we are again."

"Yes, ma'am."

Parker frowned. The teacher seemed to be the one who always accompanied the children to the ranch. She'd heard Mrs. White and Marilyn mention it a few times. Did she have her sights set on one of the cowboys? Colt maybe? Parker went to join them and introduced herself.

"Nice to meet you." Susan clapped her hands to get the attention of the group. "You're in this man's hands now. Please do not make me have to give a bad report to your parents." She smiled at Colt. "I'm strictly here to help you keep them under control."

"Me, too." Parker grinned, squaring her shoulders.

Colt gave her a strange look. "All right, guys, our first stop is the creek. Each of you grab a bucket. You'll need water. Then to the barn for fire building. If you want to eat later on, you need to be able to prepare it."

One boy raised his hand. "I need to use the bathroom."

"You're going to need to dig a hole first. Grab a shovel."

Parker's mouth fell open. Was he serious?

Colt laughed. "Outhouse is next to the barn, but you will be digging a hole today."

It took over an hour to hike to the creek and back. By the time they did, most buckets held less than half the water in them. Colt said it taught a lesson about trying to do it all at once, but it looked like a waste of time to Parker.

In the barn, the group set their buckets aside while Eric and Derrick instructed them on how to build a fire in order to purify the water and cook the hotdogs waiting for them.

Parker perched on a hay bale, more than happy to let Colt and the twins take charge.

A rustle at the back door made her glance over her shoulder. She gasped.

Mark, gun aimed at her, approached within inches, the metal touching the side of her head. "Nobody move unless I tell you." He swung his gun toward Colt who dove to the side.

Colt dropped in a heap.

Screams filled the barn.

"Quiet, or I shoot again."

"Colton!"

"Stay there, Parker," Colt said from behind a barrel. "He got me in the leg is all."

"I'll do more than that if I need to." He trained the gun at one of the twins. "Lock that back door. The other one, do the same with the front. Teacher Lady, move those kids to the far wall. On the ground, backs against the wall, legs crossed."

"How did you—" Parker gripped the edges of the hay bale.

"Get on the ranch? All it takes is for me to be smarter than the cowboys. That, and giving the dog a sleeping agent." He grinned. "Now, you, Miss Wells, are going to do exactly as I say, or do I start shooting these kids?"

Cries rose again.

"Dawson, scoot out here where I can see you!"

Colt, a bandana tied around his thigh, crawled into the open. He cut Parker a quick glance, then returned his attention to Mark. "What now?"

"I'm going to take Parker out of here. The other cowboys should be surrounding this building real soon after hearing all the screaming. Once they know I'm serious about them not interfering, Parker and I will leave. Once we reach Mexico, I'll let her go."

Mexico! She wasn't naïve enough to believe she'd live to cross the border. The man had to be lying.

Voices drifted from outside. How she wished there

was a window or two that would allow law enforcement, once they arrived, to shoot Mark. Instead, they were stuck inside this sauna of a tin can.

Parker shoved aside a strand of hair that had stuck to her cheek. She glanced back at Colt's pale face. Lines of pain creased his forehead as he scooted to rest against the wall with the kids. Blood seeped through the bandana.

"Why did you shoot Colt?" She glared.

"To take him out of the picture. If I need to, I'll make sure the next bullet puts him out permanently. Get your cell phone out."

"I don't have it."

"Don't lie to me. You never go anywhere without that thing."

She pulled her phone from her back pocket. "Now what?"

"Show me your bank balance. Then, I'll tell you where to transfer the money."

"My father put a limit on how much I can withdraw or transfer." Which wasn't a lie. She hadn't changed anything yet since his death.

"Show me." He growled.

She held up her phone. "No service in this barn." Her hand trembled.

Mark cursed and started to pace.

"I'm starting to rethink my plans to volunteer out here," Susan said loud enough for Parker to hear. "I love the horses and the atmosphere, but this ranch is trouble."

"No more so than Misty Hollow, from what I've heard." Parker set her phone on a nearby three-legged stool in case Mark ordered her to check it again. She took another look at Colt, this time their eyes locking. "What?" she mouthed.

He jerked his head toward the shovel the kids used to dig a hole. Then, he motioned at Mark.

Colt wanted her to go after the man with a shovel? Parker wasn't the physical type and, since the school had specified no guns around the students, she'd left her revolver in her house.

"Enough of this. Parker, get over here. Now," Mark growled.

One more glance at Colt, then she slid off the bale.

Mark pulled her close to his chest, , his left arm around her middle, and his right hand holding the gun to her head. "We're going to walk out that front door. If anyone tries anything, including you, I shoot you first, then one of the kids. Got it?"

"Yes." Her gaze locked with Colt's tortured one. She had so many things she wanted to say to him. How much she loved him. For him not to worry, that she'd be fine. She'd find a way to break free. He should remember and take comfort in the knowledge that she was resourceful.

His soulful eyes locked on hers. *Please don't look at me that way. You didn't fail..* Mark had known how Colt would act. That's why he'd shot him. She mouthed the words, "I love you," as Mark pushed her toward the front doors.

Chapter Nineteen

Colton's biggest fear and greatest love walked out the front door of the barn. Through the opening, he could see the rest of the ranch hands part like the Red Sea as Mark held the gun to Parker's head and passed through.

"Let me look at your leg." Susan crawled to his side.

"Tend the kids. They're scared." He brushed her hand aside and struggled to get to his feet. Once upright, he staggered toward the door and leaned heavily on the frame in time to see Mark shove Parker inside a van.

Five cowboys aimed their guns in that direction.

"No!" Colton held up his hands. "He'll kill her for sure if you start shooting."

River lowered his weapon and came to Colton's aid, propping his shoulder under Colton's arm. "Call an ambulance, somebody."

Willy whipped out his cell phone while Dylan barged into the barn.

"Thank God, no one is hurt." Colton limped to the porch assisted by River.

"You've been shot, dude."

"I meant the kids. They're shook up but unharmed. Collins shot me first thing. He meant to kill me, but I dove out of the way…kind of." He closed his eyes and leaned against the railing. "Tell me there's a tracker of Parker's phone."

"There is. We did so at the first sign of trouble, same as always, but she must've left it in the barn because that's where the signal is coming from."

How would he find her now?

Sheriff Westbrook slid his car to a halt and rushed to Colton without bothering to close his door, Deputy Hudson on his heels. "How did he get on the ranch?"

"We don't know. I haven't seen Buster." He glanced at River.

"MIA." He cleared his throat. "We thought Collins was Buster when he slipped into the barn. He's wearing the same clothes."

"You mean to tell me there's a Buster Jones somewhere without his clothes on?" The sheriff frowned. He turned to Hudson. "Check the farthest outbuilding."

"Who was on rotation?" Colt opened his eyes.

"Buster and Willy. Haven't seen him either."

"Where are the women?" The sheriff growled. "Somebody find them."

Two of the ranch hands sprinted for the main house as an ambulance roared up the drive. Soon, two paramedics tried convincing Colt to get inside.

"Not until I know Parker is safe. Tend to me here."

"Sir…" The medic glanced at the sheriff.

"I suggest you go, Dawson, but I can't force you. Be right back. There's Mrs. White." He returned a few minutes later with the news that Marilyn had gone on patrol with Buster. "Now, we have four missing people."

"Not anymore." Willy and Billy wearing nothing but boxers approached with a red-faced Marilyn.

"That man threatened my life and locked us all in an outhouse." She planted her fists on her hips. "Very tight quarters, not to mention the smell. What did we miss?" She glanced around the group.

That explained why Buster and Willy let the man take their clothes. They would've done anything to keep Marilyn safe. Colt sighed. "He's taken Parker."

"No! What about the children?"

"Safe in the barn." Colt hissed as the medic removed the bandana from around his leg.

"Bullet went clean through, but you're going to need stitches."

"Then stitch me, give me antibiotics, and leave me be." He ground the words through his teeth. "I need to find Parker."

"I've already got cars out and have notified LRPD. My bet is he'll head to her parents' house." The sheriff glanced at his car.

"He said Mexico."

"Mexico?"

"Yep. Something about her giving him money and him letting her go when they reach Mexico. She'll never make it there alive." Colt winced as the medic poured disinfectant over his wound. Could the man move any slower?

Hudson and Dylan escorted the teacher and students from the barn and into the house. Colt's heart might have dropped to his knees at Parker's abduction, but things could've been a lot worse. He'd find Parker.

He would. She was a smart woman. She'd find a way to stay alive until he found her. Hope was all he had.

Sheriff Westbrook strode toward his vehicle.

"Wait up." Colt pulled himself to his feet. "I'm coming with you."

"No, it's best you stay here." The sheriff kept going.

"I'll follow." Colt hobbled after him.

"Dude…" River shot out a hand to stop him.

Colt whipped around. "Do not stop me."

"Okay." He put his hands up. "Call if there's anything we can do from here."

"You can count on it." Colt shuffled faster, reached the car, and yanked the passenger side door open.

The sheriff shook his head. "Don't do anything foolish."

"I won't." He pounded the hood of the car. "I need a gun."

"That is exactly what I'm talking about." The sheriff turned the key in the ignition as

Maverick brought him a gun and an extra clip. "Good luck, man." He stepped back.

"Thanks." Colt slid onto the seat and clicked his seatbelt into place. "Drive like it's your wife we're after."

The sheriff narrowed his eyes. "Look, I want to get Parker back safe as much as you do. Now sit there and let me do my job. And don't do anything stupid."

~

As soon as they were out of sight of the ranch, Mark turned onto a side road and pulled the van over into a break in the woods. He ordered Parker into the back of the van where he handcuffed her to a bar attached to the wall. Then, he got back into the driver's seat and sped down the mountain at a speed that kept Parker's heart pounding.

She scanned the back of the van for a weapon or anything that would help her get free. A tire iron lay against the far wall out of reach. A couple of boxes slid when the van careened around a corner.

A cry escaped her as she slammed against the wall on a hairpin curve. "Slow down. You won't get any money if I'm dead."

"Shut up. I need to concentrate."

"Where are we going?"

"I said. Shut. Up."

Tires squealed as they rounded another corner.

Parker tried to sit, but the pain in her wrist from the handcuff made it impossible. Another curve and another slam to the wall. This time she landed on her elbow, which knocked the breath from her lungs.

Had Colt received medical attention? How did Mark get on the ranch? Questions tumbled through her mind aching to be released.

"Thank you for not shooting any of the children." Maybe she could appeal to the human side of Mark. Help him see reason. Get him to let her go after she gave him the money. It was only money. All she wanted was a life with Colt. She couldn't have that if she were dead.

"Wish I'd killed the cowboy." He set his gun on the passenger seat.

Rage boiled through her, and she aimed a kick at the back of the driver's seat, but her legs weren't long enough.

"You should be glad you didn't add another

murder to the list." She tried to stretch her leg to reach the crowbar.

"What's one more dead body? If I get caught, which I won't, one more won't increase my prison time much."

They exited off the mountain and sped down Main Street before rocketing onto the interstate.

"Are we really going all the way to Mexico?"

"Yep. Best place I know to hide and live the easy life on a hundred grand. I'll find a place to hole up long enough for you to get me my money, then on we go."

"That's going to be difficult. I left my phone at the ranch."

He glared through the rearview mirror. "You have to be the dumbest woman I've ever met."

Or the smartest. She ducked her head and grinned. Now, he'd have to either find her another phone or stop at a bank. Both would take time which would allow Colt to get closer. She had no doubt he'd be coming for her, gunshot or not.

Mark cursed and pounded the steering wheel, muttering about needing a new plan.

Good. Parker would do her best to foil any plan he came up with.

First, she needed to distract him enough to get a hold of that gun. "Can you get me a phone?"

"I'm thinking."

"I could log in on yours."

"You'd like that, wouldn't you?" He peered in the rearview mirror again. "I'm sure you know a way to do that so they can track us."

"I'm no techno-geek." She forced a laugh, trying to sound lighthearted and foolish despite the fear coursing through her. If he actually believed her to be dumb, it might work in her favor. "How did you get on the ranch? We thought we had everything covered."

He laughed. "I'm smarter than you and a bunch of cowboys. Most men will do anything to protect the woman they love, even give me their clothes."

She frowned. "I don't know what that means."

"I took that Buster guy's clothes by threatening to shoot the woman he cares for. We're the same build. All I had to do was keep my head down and waltz into that barn. Brilliant. See? That's why I'm going to get what I want. I've thought through every possible scenario."

Keep bragging. You've never dealt with Parker Wells before. She had *always* gotten what she wanted. "Those kids sure were excited about building a fire to cook their own hotdogs. Too bad they won't be able to do that. You probably traumatized them for life."

"Good. I don't like kids."

"How can you not like kids? It must be because you haven't been around them. I used to feel the same way, but working on the ranch has given me a new understanding of what's important in life." She tried again to reach the tire iron.

"Oh, yeah? Like what?"

"People. Love. Not investing in the rat race. Take you, for example." The handcuff bit into her skin as she stretched. "Money's all you care about. Why do you need it so bad?"

"A question from someone who's never been without." Derision dripped from his words.

"I can't help it because I was born to parents with money. My father worked hard for what he had." She gave up, tears springing to her eyes. The iron was only inches from her foot. A mile of inches.

Despair swelled. What if she didn't find a way free? What if Colt was injured more than she thought and couldn't come for her? What if the sheriff couldn't find her in time?

"You've gone quiet," Mark said.

She sniffed. "Leave me alone."

"Are you crying?"

"No." Almost. She took a deep breath. She wouldn't give him the satisfaction of knowing how frightened she was.

"I'm not going to drive all the way to Mexico with some whiny, sniveling woman. Chin up, or I'll dump your body somewhere no one will be able to find you."

Heartless man. "I'm entitled to a few moments of self-pity. In that note you said you once wanted to marry me. What happened?"

"Your father refused my request. Accused me of stealing from the company."

"Weren't you?"

"Yeah. Your point? I wouldn't have had to embezzle funds if I'd married you."

"I didn't know you existed." The man was delusional.

"That could've been easily remedied. Had he not said no, made accusations and threats, your parents would still be alive. It's really all your father's fault, you see."

"What do you so desperately need money for that you'd commit murder?"

He shrugged. "At first, it was to pay for my mother's medical bills, but it's too late for her now. It's all about revenge. Plain, simple revenge toward the family that ruined my life…and hers."

Chapter Twenty

Parker quieted, stunned, and stared at the back of Mark's head for several seconds. "I'm very sorry about your mother, but stealing is wrong, no matter how you look at it. If you'd bothered to speak to my father—"

"You stupid, naïve, spoiled little rich girl! She'll never get better. Your father didn't care a bit about my mother." Spittle from his lips hit the windshield.

"You don't know that because you didn't ask," she said softly. Her parents would've helped. She knew that deep in her heart. "Now, because of your crimes of stealing and murder, your mother will die. I feel sorry for you."

"Shut up! I don't want you feeling anything for me but fear." The van swerved. A passing vehicle honked.

Parker yanked harder on the handcuffs, curling her hand as small as she could make it, biting back a cry at the pain. She had to get out of the van. Parker started yelling and banging the walls. One of the boxes had scooted closer when the van swerved. She opened it to discover cleaning rags.

One by one she held them up. The wind from the open passenger window grabbed them and they flew out. She then tried to stretch to kick out the back light, but her legs weren't long enough.

Mark cursed and swatted his arm behind him as he might at a disobedient child in the back seat. "When we stop, I'm going to make you regret this."

"And I regret the day you were born." She regretted the words the instant they left her mouth.

Mark reached for his gun and fired behind him.

The bullet flew past her head and punctured a hole in the back door.

Parker flinched at the sound of screeching tires. Hopefully, someone would call the police. "Don't endanger anyone else."

"Then, behave so I won't have to."

The back of the van grew sweltering. Parker's mouth turned to cotton. Her head pounded. Her wrist burned. She gave the bar he'd hooked her to a couple of kicks before sitting back.

I can't give up. There has to be a way to get free. All she needed to do was think on it a bit more. She chewed the fingernail on her left hand. The rags must have attracted some attention. The gunshot would've helped, too. Somebody would call for help. All she had to do was stay alive long enough. Mark had to stop for gas or to rest at some point. She'd make her move then.

The van swerved again. A cigarette lighter slid across the floor of the van. She snorted. Why couldn't the tire iron slide her way? She flicked the lighter, smiling at the tiny flame, then slid it into her pocket before studying the van floor for any other loose items.

She eyed the tire iron again. If the van swerved hard enough… She stretched to kick the back of Mark's seat again. The most she could do was irritate him.

When he threatened to shoot again, she inched back. "Where is your mother now?"

"You already know that. I told you when I ran into you in Little Rock."

"You do realize that you'll be going to jail, right? Your mother will die alone, even if you do make it to Mexico. They won't let you return to the states. You've accomplished nothing."

"I'll be a rich man."

"Are you serious? I'm not going to be able to waltz into a bank and withdraw all my money. That's not how banks work."

He glanced over his shoulder. "That's why you're going with me until we can find a way to transfer the money to an offshore account." Narrow eyes glared at her in the rearview mirror.

"You watch too much television."

"Are you trying to make me kill you sooner?"

She shrugged and leaned her head back, closing her eyes. *Come on, Colton, and bring the sheriff's department with you.*

Her eyes popped open when the van slowed, then stopped. She must have fallen asleep because the day had turned dusky. Her stomach growled as the smell of hotdogs drifted in the window.

Mark turned in his seat. "Make one little sound, and I'll shoot the nearest person, then another and another until you figure it out. Understand? This is going to be a quick trip."

"I'm thirty, I'm hungry, and I need to use the restroom."

He cursed again. "I mean it, Parker. I'll take you inside, but you'd better behave yourself."

"Promise." She flashed a smile and smoothed back her perspiration-soaked hair.

After unlocking the back door and the cuffs, he pulled her close. "We're in love, got it? On our way to our honeymoon in Rocky Point, Mexico. Visiting some sights on the way. Don't speak. Understood?"

"Yes." Her legs threatened to buckle after having sat for so long, but she forced them to straighten as they moved toward the gas station doors. She spotted the sign for the bathrooms and nudged Mark.

"I'll be waiting right outside." His features hardened.

Unfortunately, the bathroom had one toilet and no window or other means of escape. Nobody could help her once she was back in the van. She quickly took care of business and washed her face and hands. When she'd stalled enough, and Mark pounded on the door, she stepped out.

"A hotdog and a bottle of water, please."

"Fine. Remember what I told you." He pinched her waist, then pasted on a grin. "Two hot dogs, one water, and the tallest coffee you got."

"Coffee is self-serve," the cashier said. "So are the hot dogs. Condiments next to them." The young man barely glanced up.

Mark huffed, then pulled Parker to the hot dogs. "Get two. Onions and mustard on mine. I'll get my coffee."

She raised her eyebrows. He was releasing his hold on her? *Thank you, God.*

Without a backward glance, she darted for the door. "Call the police! I've been kidnapped." She slammed the door behind her and ran across the lot toward the interstate. If she were lucky, she could get a truck driver to stop and give her a ride.

"Hey!" Mark shouted behind her.

Parker glanced over her shoulder and stumbled.

Cars whipped between them, one stopping to block his way, then speeding ahead when Mark aimed his gun.

It gave Parker a few seconds' lead.

Horns blared as she dashed onto the shoulder of the interstate. Seeing Mark gaining ground, she dove into the ditch, then scrambled into a thick stand of trees and under a barbed-wire fence. Her small size gave her an advantage—she could easily scoot under places he would have to struggle to get through.

She emerged from the pasture by skirting under another portion of barbed-wire fence and onto a less-traveled highway. Help would be slim this time of the evening. She needed to make her way back to the interstate. Colt and the sheriff wouldn't find her on a side road.

She stopped to catch her breath, holding a hand to the stitch in her side, and listened for the sounds of traffic. The screech of brakes had her turning left. Using the fence to guide her through the quickly falling night, she ran as fast as she could back toward the sounds of traffic.

Where was Mark? Her heart pounded in her throat. He could hide and shoot her as she passed, and she wouldn't know until the bullet pierced her skin.

Poor Colton. He would never get over her death or his failure to protect her. Parker had to survive for his sake and for her own. She hadn't told him of her plans for their future. All she could do was hope and pray she survived and that he wanted the same future she did.

A rustling in the brush made her freeze in place. Her heart rate increased, then slowed as a black cow poked his head out.

"You scared me, silly girl," Parker whispered. "Don't give me away, okay?"

Her stomach rumbled, reminding her she'd left her supper behind. Why couldn't she have at least fled with the bottle of water? Continuing on her way, she pushed aside her lightheadedness at not having drunk anything for hours.

Her legs grew heavy. The ditch between her and the interstate seemed insurmountable. But, she couldn't stop. Not until she reached freedom. She struggled up the steep incline, pausing for a moment at the top, her breath coming in loud gasps.

Far ahead of her, lights flashed. Help was on its way!

Parker found energy from deep inside herself and started to run.

"I will shoot you, Parker Wells! I don't care about the money anymore. All I want is every Wells family member dead."

She glanced back to see Mark climbing up the embankment mere yards behind her. He was too far away to make an accurate shot with a handgun. Tossing a prayer heavenward, she pulled on the last of her resources and increased her speed.

~

Colt's heart almost stopped at the sight of Parker sprinting down the shoulder of the interstate. "Pull over!"

"I see her." The sheriff cut across the median,

causing cars and trucks to honk and swerve, and stopped a few yards from Parker. "Collins is catching up fast." He shoved his gun open. "Get your woman. I'll take care of him."

Colt took a deep breath and struggled to his feet. Leaning heavily on the hood of the car, he pushed away and stumbled toward Parker.

"No." She waved her arms. "Get back inside. He'll shoot you." She joined Colt behind the open front door, then looked back to see Mark stop, take aim, and miss.

He whipped around and hightailed it in the other direction, Sheriff Westbrook giving chase. Seconds later, another deputy's car cut him off, and Hudson aimed his weapon out the window.

It was done. Colt opened his arms and enveloped her in them. Parker wrapped hers around his neck and buried her face. "Thank God. I've never been so scared in my life."

"I'm pretty sure my fear can beat yours, sweetheart." She'd never felt so good to him.

"Are the kids okay? Anyone hurt?" She lifted her head to stare into his eyes.

"Everyone is fine. A little shook up is all."

"You?"

"Stitched up. I'll be fine. Let's get in the car and wait for the sheriff." His leg was losing the battle to support his weight. He opened the back door and let her slide in first. A sigh of relief escaped him as he joined her.

"You aren't fine. Liar. You're in pain."

He grimaced as he shifted in the seat. "You're going to be right, but I'm relieved that you're back with me." He smiled and leaned his head back, putting his arm around her shoulders and tucking her into his side.

"Do you have anything to eat or drink? I'm starving."

He laughed and climbed back out of the car, grateful the sheriff's department didn't have doors in the back that couldn't be opened from the inside. He retrieved a bottle of water from the console and dug in the glove compartment for food. Nothing.

"Sorry. This is it." He handed her the water as he struggled back into the car.

She guzzled half of it in one try. "That's better."

Through the windshield, Colt watched as the sheriff and Deputy Hudson cuffed Collins and put him in the back of Hudson's car. When they'd done so, the sheriff returned to Colt and Parker.

"You okay?" He bent and peered in the back.

"Yes. I am now. The van is at a gas station…not sure how far ahead. I lost track of the time."

"We know where it is. The 911 operator received a lot of calls." He grinned. "Good thinking on your part, Parker. The cashier said as soon as Collins turned around, you took off like a rocket."

"I didn't know if I'd get another chance." She scooted against Colt again. "I'm ready to go back to the ranch, Sheriff."

"I'm ready, too." Colt kissed the top of her head, more relieved than he'd ever been before. Tonight could have ended so differently.

Epilogue

Six months later

Colton smiled at her. "Where are we going?"

"Pull over."

He frowned. "On the side of the mountain?"

"There are no cars coming, and I need to blindfold you and take it from here." She grinned.

He turned off the engine. "I'm not crazy about this."

"It's a surprise. Don't ruin it." She gave his arm a playful slap. "Now get out and let me do this."

"It's cold outside." His smile widened, but he did as she asked.

She joined him and slipped a sleep mask over his eyes. "Duck your head and get in the passenger seat."

"Yes, ma'am." He climbed inside. "I'm at your mercy."

She giggled. "Yes, you are. I'm going to take advantage of this." She leaned over and gave him a kiss before taking over the driving.

A short distance down the road, she found a place wide enough to turn around and headed back down the mountain instead of up.

"Okay, I'm intrigued. I thought we were going home."

"We are. Just relax." Parker had done a lot of planning during the last few months, which hadn't been easy since Colt rarely let her out of his sight. If not for heading into town with Mrs. White on occasion, then slipping away with the woman's help, she might not have accomplished anything.

She drove through the town of Misty Hollow to the valley. A few careful questions to Dylan had sent her in the right direction. Her heart lodged in her throat. Oh, how she hoped Colt would be pleased. She pulled over and turned off the ignition. "Wait there. Let me help you out."

"Can't I take off the blindfold?"

"In a minute." She rushed from the car and to the passenger's side where she helped him out. Then, positioning him where she wanted him to stand, she whipped off the mask.

He glanced at the field, then the For Sale sign that now said Sold. "I don't understand."

"Isn't this the land you wanted?"

"Yes, but it's sold. How did you know?"

"Dylan told me." She grinned and clapped her hands. "Have you looked at the small farmhouse on the land? It's perfect for the time being."

"Parker, I don't understand what's happening." His frown deepened.

She took a deep breath. "I sold my parents' house and bought this land for you. We can live in that little farmhouse while you buy cattle." She took his hands in hers, his features blurring through her tears. "I'm so sorry for all I put you through over the last year. Will you marry me and let me make it up to you? I don't want a big wedding. My parents aren't here to celebrate with us. Something simple on the ranch is fine."

He put a finger to her lips. "You bought this for *me*?" His eyes brimmed. "For us?"

"If you'll have me." *Oh, please say yes.* "I know it isn't traditional for the woman to ask—"

He pulled free of her grasp and cupped her head. "You crazy, insane woman. Yes, I'll marry you, and we'll raise a herd of kids and cattle on this land while I build you the perfect house."

"The perfect house is the one that has you living in it with me." Tears trickled down her cheeks.

He wiped them away with his thumbs, then lowered his head, and claimed her lips with his. When they were both breathless, he stepped back. "Let's go get married. Right now at the Justice of the Peace. We can have a reception at the ranch in a couple of days. I don't want to spend one more night without you. If you want a big wedding—"

"I don't. All I want is you." She couldn't think of a more romantic plan.

The End

Dear Reader,

I hope you are enjoying this new series as much as I am enjoying writing it. Who doesn't love a cowboy? Especially a wounded one looking for love?

If you enjoyed this book, please head to Amazon and leave a review or a rating. It doesn't have to be a long one, but reviews are very important to authors.

God Bless,

Cynthia

www.cynthiahickey.com

Cynthia Hickey is a multi-published and best-selling author of cozy mysteries and romantic suspense. She has taught writing at many conferences and small writing retreats. She and her husband run the publishing press, Winged Publications. They live in Arizona and Arkansas, becoming snowbirds with three dogs. They have ten grandchildren who keep them busy and tell everyone they know that "Nana is a writer."

Connect with me on FaceBook
Twitter
Sign up for my newsletter and receive a free short story
www.cynthiahickey.com

Follow me on Amazon
And Bookbub
Shop my bookstore on shopify. For better prices and autographed books.

Enjoy other books by Cynthia Hickey

Cowboys of Misty Hollow
Cowboy Jeopardy

Misty Hollow
Secrets of Misty Hollow
Deceptive Peace
Calm Surface
Lightning Never Strikes Twice
Lethal Inheritance
Bitter Isolation
Say I Don't
Christmas Stalker
Bridge to Safety
When Night Falls
A Place to Hide
Mountain Refuge

Stay in Misty Hollow for a while. Get the entire series here!

The Seven Deadly Sins series
Deadly Pride
Deadly Covet
Deadly Lust
Deadly Glutton
Deadly Envy
Deadly Sloth
Deadly Anger

The Tail Waggin' Mysteries
Cat-Eyed Witness
The Dog Who Found a Body
Troublesome Twosome
Four-Legged Suspect
Unwanted Christmas Guest

Wedding Day Cat Burglar

Brothers Steele
Sharp as Steele
Carved in Steele
Forged in Steele
Brothers Steele (All three in one)

The Brothers of Copper Pass
Wyatt's Warrant
Dirk's Defense
Stetson's Secret
Houston's Hope
Dallas's Dare
Seth's Sacrifice
Malcolm's Misunderstanding
The Brothers of Copper Pass Boxed Set

Time Travel
The Portal

Tiny House Mysteries
No Small Caper
Caper Goes Missing
Caper Finds a Clue
Caper's Dark Adventure
A Strange Game for Caper
Caper Steals Christmas
Caper Finds a Treasure
Tiny House Mysteries boxed set

Wife for Hire – Private Investigators
Saving Sarah
Lesson for Lacey
Mission for Meghan
Long Way for Lainie
Aimed at Amy
Wife for Hire (all five in one)

A Hollywood Murder
Killer Pose, book 1
Killer Snapshot, book 2
Shoot to Kill, book 3
Kodak Kill Shot, book 4
To Snap a Killer
Hollywood Murder Mysteries

Shady Acres Mysteries
Beware the Orchids, book 1
Path to Nowhere
Poison Foliage
Poinsettia Madness
Deadly Greenhouse Gases
Vine Entrapment
Shady Acres Boxed Set

CLEAN BUT GRITTY Romantic Suspense

Highland Springs

Murder Live
Say Bye to Mommy
To Breathe Again

Highland Springs Murders (all 3 in one)

Colors of Evil Series

Shades of Crimson
Coral Shadows

The Pretty Must Die Series

Ripped in Red, book 1
Pierced in Pink, book 2
Wounded in White, book 3
Worthy, The Complete Story

Lisa Paxton Mystery Series

Eenie Meenie Miny Mo
Jack Be Nimble
Hickory Dickory Dock
Boxed Set

Hearts of Courage
A Heart of Valor
The Game
Suspicious Minds
After the Storm
Local Betrayal
Hearts of Courage Boxed Set

Overcoming Evil series
Mistaken Assassin
Captured Innocence

Mountain of Fear
Exposure at Sea
A Secret to Die for
Collision Course
Romantic Suspense of 5 books in 1

INSPIRATIONAL

Nosy Neighbor Series
Anything For A Mystery, Book 1
A Killer Plot, Book 2
Skin Care Can Be Murder, Book 3
Death By Baking, Book 4
Jogging Is Bad For Your Health, Book 5
Poison Bubbles, Book 6
A Good Party Can Kill You, Book 7
Nosy Neighbor collection

Christmas with Stormi Nelson

The Summer Meadows Series
Fudge-Laced Felonies, Book 1
Candy-Coated Secrets, Book 2
Chocolate-Covered Crime, Book 3
Maui Macadamia Madness, Book 4
All four novels in one collection

The River Valley Mystery Series
Deadly Neighbors, Book 1
Advance Notice, Book 2
The Librarian's Last Chapter, Book 3

All three novels in one collection

Made in the USA
Monee, IL
03 May 2024